The Lake

The Lake of the Bees

Theodor Storm

Translated by Jonathan Katz

ET REMOTISSIMA PROPE

100 PAGES

100 PAGES
Published by Hesperus Press Limited
4 Rickett Street, London SW6 1RU
www.hesperuspress.com

The Lake of the Bees first published in German as *Immensee* in 1850;
A Quiet Musician first published in German as *Ein stiller Musikant* in 1875
This translation first published by Hesperus Press Limited, 2003

Designed and typeset by Fraser Muggeridge
Printed in the United Arab Emirates by Oriental Press

ISBN: 1-84391-044-6

CONTENTS

FOREWORD

I once had the notion of choosing the seven best short stories of the world as a personal anthology which might interest a publisher, but the titles listed in a notebook lacked the love story it seemed essential to include. I was too busy writing novels and nothing came of the idea, but reading *The Lake of the Bees*, it was obvious that the magical narration of an elderly man, recreating the love of his life from childhood to youth, was a story that would have been included.

Reinhard is about twice the age of five-year-old Elisabeth, an unusual discrepancy in years for a childhood friendship, but they share fantasies, as when he says they'll one day go to India together. Viewing their association as lasting for life, he wonders whether she will be brave enough to break all bonds and go with him.

Spending most of their time together, he protects her at school from the teacher's displeasure, and copies into his notebook a poem he keeps to himself. At seventeen he leaves for a school in another town, and though the intensity of the relationship seems greater on his side than on hers, he fervently believes in it. A gypsy girl in a tavern sings: 'But this one day I am so fair', which he sees as relevant to his influence over Elisabeth. The gypsy girl appears later in the story: 'dressed in rags', with 'the signs of a beauty now lost', as if to taunt him with the loss of his love.

Impelled back to his lodgings he finds a letter from Elisabeth in which she chides him for failing to send stories from the notebook as promised, also telling him that Erich, a mutual friend, has been calling at the house to see her.

Incidents which Reinhard only half understands occur as recollections when it is too late. He goes home at Easter to find his sweetheart changed. The linnet he gave her had died in his absence, and has been replaced by a bird from Erich. He no longer finds the same favour in her mother's eyes, because Erich, who will inherit his father's estate at Immensee, will make a better match for her daughter.

When Elisabeth and Reinhard go walking, collecting botanical specimens, he seems to have no will, no energy to make decisions, though in that respect both are equally weak. He can't realise that to say yes rather than no is less demanding, that there is always energy to deal with what saying yes leads to, and that though the movements of the heart may be controlled by a metronome dancing fast or slow, the touch of a finger can push the whole thing over.

As is often the case with those who exist in a dream, Reinhard takes too much for granted. Falling in love as a child was so natural it seems inconceivable that it can ever change, though when hearing of Erich's attentions to Elisabeth, hardly realising that it is always a friend who captures your loved one, 'in his eyes there was a sudden expression of sadness which she had never seen there', and his only response is that he, 'can't stand that yellow bird' that Erich has given her.

Elisabeth sees him off at the coach station when he is leaving for two more years, and he wants to say something, 'on which depended all the worth and all the sweetness of his future life; and yet he could not find the words'. She tells him that she has defended him from her mother who said he had changed for the worse, and he can only reply that he was just the same as he always had been.

Some years later Reinhard sets out for Immensee, where Erich lives with Elisabeth on the farm he inherited. Erich is friendly and hospitable, as he can now afford to be, though conscious of the past relationship between Reinhard and his wife.

Not having been told of the visit, Elisabeth is shocked to see her old sweetheart, and Reinhard feels, 'a sharp burst of pain in his heart'. Erich, the puppet-master who puts their destinies at risk, says of Reinhard: 'we won't let him go so soon', perhaps to tempt them into an elopement, though certain his wife could take no such course; or he thinks that the longer Reinhard is with them the more chance there will be of Elisabeth forgetting the love of her childhood.

The story is leisured and precise, its hypnotic prose bringing speculation continually to mind, the account of a lifetime coming at its own pace, almost writing itself in the way a masterpiece sometimes is produced, never a note wrong, or a word to jar. The dreamlike accuracy of each scene flows into the next, everything said suggesting the weight of so much left unsaid, emotions subliminally felt rather than stated, until the heartbreaking chronicle is complete.

Elisabeth and Reinhard sing Tyrolese folk songs together, and Erich's reaction is that of a boor: they're just 'little ditties' written by 'common rabble', and he sits in silence with folded arms at Elisabeth's 'slightly reticent contralto' when she and Reinhard sing a song from their childhood.

Reinhard swims towards a phantom lily in the lake, which he can never reach, and his lack of success makes the prosaic Erich wonder, 'what the devil did you want with the water lily?' not knowing it was a glimpse of Elisabeth out in a rainstorm looking for him. Still in love – indicated by a letter she leaves for him to see – they had been unable to find each other. A lifetime is needed to master the rules of love, at least by those who barely understand them in the first place, and by then, as the old man telling the story knows, it is far too late.

A storyteller recreates the past to get as close to the truth as possible, yet one wonders why Elisabeth and Reinhard don't embrace and go away to that India talked of in childhood; and while you know they won't, because of the solitary old man and his story, you still hope that by some subterfuge of the author's narration they will do so, Reinhard already having recognised Elisabeth as a 'once lively child', who nevertheless 'had surely promised to be less subdued as a grown woman'.

Too often one doesn't embrace, misses the chance, refuses the challenge, denies destiny, and it is the failure to respond at such moments that makes memory more precious than any action – the theme that endows *The Lake of the Bees* with its quality of genius.

– *Alan Sillitoe, 2003*

INTRODUCTION

The short prose narrative form which came to be known as the '*Novelle*' was one of the most compelling and enduring genres in nineteenth-century German literature. At a particularly high point in its development stand a group of writers now collectively associated with the movement of 'Poetic Realism', and prominent among them was a native of Husum, a small coastal town in the far northern province of Schleswig.

Theodor Woldsen Storm was born in 1817, the son of a successful and locally respected lawyer, Johann Casimir Storm. His mother, Lucie Woldsen, came from one of the leading merchant families of the region. Theodor enjoyed a happy childhood amidst prosperous respectability and a large family. There was, however, an incipient melancholy in the boy, and many of the autobiographical and nostalgic themes in his poetry and prose writings may be attributed to the interaction of this sensitivity with a strong childhood influence of storytelling. Chief among those he heard was a sister of the Storms' family servant and nurse, a lady he later referred to as 'Lena Wies'. From her and others he was exposed to the charm of narrative and, no doubt, the suggestive power of language. Bilingual in the local Low German and in High German, he absorbed much of the lore and customs of the region. His own literary inclinations began to emerge, and when he left Husum at the age of seventeen to continue his schooling in Lübeck, and subsequently as a law student at the University of Kiel and in Berlin, he came under the influence of writers and scholars – including the Mommsen brothers Tycho and Theodor – who stimulated his interests and talents. The fruits of their friendship and collaboration are to be found in the *Liederbuch dreier Freunde* ('Songbook of Three Friends'), an anthology of poems and ballads which they collected in Schleswig-Holstein and published in 1843. Qualifying in 1842, Storm had returned to Husum to begin his career as a lawyer.

During the first year of his higher studies he appears to have experienced his first love; at the age of nineteen he fell in love with Bertha von Buchan, who was at the time almost eleven years old. Some years later she rejected his proposal of marriage. The relationship had been innocent, and largely one-sided. Significantly, Theodor sent her letters and wrote stories and poems for her; she was clearly the inspiration behind the character of Elisabeth in his first major success as a prose writer, *Immensee* (written in 1849 and published in its first version in 1850).

As a young professional in Husum, Storm busily involved himself in the life of the town. A popular figure in the community, he took part in theatrical productions and, following his passionate musical interests, founded and directed an active and successful choral society. A year after his rejection by Bertha he was engaged to a cousin, Constanze Esmarch, whom he married in 1846. Later letters reveal that personal problems hung over their earliest years together. In 1847 Storm was in love with a young admirer, Dorothea Jensen; this strong attraction supplied, in his own words, the 'passion' that was at first lacking in his love for Constanze. The marriage was however strengthened by the birth of their first child, Hans, in 1848. It was in the late 1840s that Theodor turned his literary talents to prose fiction, though he also continued to write and publish poetry till his final days.

At this time also political events brought considerable upheaval to the life of Husum and the entire region. The Danish intervention in Schleswig in 1850, and consequent cultural and administrative changes, eventually caused Storm to leave Husum for a post in the Prussian judiciary at Potsdam in 1853, where he was shortly followed by his wife and three young sons. In 1856 they moved on to a more satisfactory life in the small Thuringian town of Heiligenstadt, where he had obtained a post as District Magistrate. A daughter was born in 1855 in Potsdam, and two further daughters in Heiligenstadt.

The Storms' return to Husum followed immediately on Bismarck's settlement of the Schleswig-Holstein problem in 1864. Theodor first took a senior administrative post in the judiciary, and then in 1866, under the imposition of Prussian rule and a revised constitution, he took a lower-paid and less satisfactory position as District Judge. In the meantime, tragedy had struck with Constanze's death during the birth of their fourth daughter in 1865. In June 1866 Theodor married Dorothea Jensen, and a daughter was born to them in 1868. After these years of personal complications and sorrows in Storm's life, during which he had had less time for creative work, he found greater stability and returned to a routine of writing. During the 1870s he produced a large number of highly accomplished *Novellen*. His talents remained with him, and indeed developed, to the end; after his retirement in 1880, in particular, and his move to a house his father had owned in the Holstein village of Hademarschen a few miles from Husum, he continued to write. He had by this time attained national fame as a literary figure and great respect among his fellow writers. It was in 1888, the last year of his life, that Storm finished the work that is commonly regarded as his finest *Novelle* of all, *Der Schimmelreiter* [*The Rider on the White Horse*], an immensely powerful and atmospheric tale of life on the Friesian coast.

It was, famously, Theodor Storm's own observation that his '*Novellendichtung*' was an offshoot of his lyric poetry.

'Lyric', 'poetic realism', even the term '*Novelle*' itself, have perhaps been over-zealously defined in critical literature, but the poetic force of Storm's prose is never in doubt. It is almost as if the narrative form liberated his most evocative language. The two stories in the present volume may be seen to illustrate this affinity in various ways. The language is effortlessly fluent and 'rhythmic', and yet carefully chosen for its suggestive power; symbols abound, situations recall memories, words summon associations. Atmosphere, mood ('*Stimmung*'), the ecphrastic painting of scenes and settings in which human drama and emotions are played out, have often a generalising effect and, however individual the character depictions may be, the reader is repeatedly drawn to contemplate human conditions, traits and foibles. The situations are often paradigms, and for this reason we forgive, or indeed disregard, some implausible occurrences. Certain key words act as talismans – the reader will find his own; in the second story it is above all the word '*still*' ('quiet') of the title itself that recurs frequently and each time invites a new contemplation of the loveable old musician's temperament and circumstances. Another talisman is the model of the folk song itself; it would be hard to find a more beautiful description of the nature of folk literature than that given in *The Lake of the Bees* by Reinhard, in his rebuttal of Erich's obtuse and dismissive characterisation of the songs as 'ditties':

> 'They are not composed at all; they grow, they fall from the air, they fly over the land like gossamer, here, there, everywhere, and are sung in a thousand places at once. It is our innermost feelings and sufferings we find in these songs; it is as if we all had a hand in creating them.'

In Storm's case there are strong links between personal experience and his creative writing. His letters to friends, and accounts of his life, throw much light on the genesis of both his plots and his language. The two stories here are to some extent complementary; they both deal with personal sadness and frustration, but the balance of pain and optimism is different in each. Storm's touching sympathy with the lonely or marginal figure in society is focused on the artist. In each case it is through simple lyric that the artist's inner understanding of himself and the world is expressed. In each case we are shown the genesis of the character's own poetic thoughts. *Ein stiller Musikant* ['A Quiet Musucian'] was published in 1875. In 1863 the Storms' third son, the teenager Karl, a troubled soul who like his older brother Hans was to cause his father intense anxiety, went for a walk in the hills near Heiligenstadt and came back with a lyric poem for his father. Theodor treasured the poem and used some of it in the crucial composition in his story more than a decade later. Like Christian Valentin in the story, Karl became a music teacher. But Valentin's moving boyhood reconciliation after the devastating encounter with his father's wrath, and his coming to terms with his own limitations ('life has dealt with me tolerably well') are a 'projection' and wish-fulfilment on the author's part. This is one among several of Storm's stories that touch on the complexities of father-son relations. It was doubtless his intention that it should touch the hearts of both fathers and sons.

– Jonathan Katz, 2003

Note on the Text:

The little poetic meditation on nostalgia and loss that stands at the head of *The Lake of the Bees* was written by Storm in late 1856 for the illustrated edition. It was included by J.M. Ritchie in his excellent edition of the German text (London, 1969). It is Ritchie's text that I have used for this translation, and that of the *Sämtliche Werke* ['Collected Works'], edited by Christian Jenssen (Wiesbaden, n.d.), for 'A Quiet Musician'.

The Lake of the Bees

These leaves breathe forth the scent of violets
That grew at home upon my childhood's field;
From year to year they came, yet no one knew,
And I to memory alone must yield.

The Old Man

One afternoon in late autumn an elderly, well-dressed man was making his way slowly down the road. He seemed to be on his way home after a walk; his buckled shoes, of a style now long out of fashion, were dusty from the road, and he carried his long, gold-topped stick under his arm. His dark eyes, which seemed the last refuge of his lost youth, and contrasted curiously with his snow-white hair, looked calmly around and down into the town that lay below him in the haze of the evening sun. He seemed almost a stranger; few who passed greeted him, though several were compelled to gaze involuntarily into those serious eyes.

At last he stopped before a high, gabled house, took one more look out at the town, and stepped through a doorway into the hall. As the bell rang, a green curtain was drawn back from the peep-hole window of a room which led off the hall, and behind it was revealed the face of an old woman.

The man signalled to her with his stick. 'No lamps lit yet!' he said, in a slightly southern accent, and the housekeeper let go of the curtain again.

The old man crossed the wide entrance hall and passed through a downstairs room, where large oak dressers with china vases stood against the walls. Then, opening a door on the other side, he entered a small corridor, from which a narrow staircase rose to the upper rooms at the back of the house. Climbing the steps slowly, he opened another door at the top and stepped into a medium-sized room. It was cosy and quiet here, with one wall almost completely covered with shelves and bookcases, and another hung with paintings and portraits. On a green-covered table lay a number of open books, and before it stood a heavy armchair with a red velvet cushion. The old man put his hat and stick in the corner and sat down in the armchair; with his hands folded, he seemed to be resting after his walk.

As he sat there, it grew gradually darker, until at last a shaft of moonlight shone through the window-pane and fell upon the paintings on the wall; his eyes instinctively followed as the bright beam moved slowly along. Presently it travelled over a small picture in a plain black frame.

'Elisabeth!' said the old man softly. And as he spoke, time shifted and he found himself once more in the days of his youth.

Before long the charming figure of a small girl came to him. Her name was Elisabeth, and she was around five years old. He himself was twice her age. Around her neck she wore a little kerchief of red silk, and it looked pretty next to her brown eyes.

'Reinhard!' she called, 'we've no school today – no school! We have the whole day free, and tomorrow too!'

Straight away Reinhard put the slate he was carrying under his arm behind the front door, and the two children ran through the house into the garden and out through the garden gate into the meadow beyond. This unexpected holiday suited them marvellously well. With Elisabeth's help Reinhard had built a little turf house where they were going to spend their summer evenings. All that was missing was a seat, and Reinhard immediately got to work; hammer, nails, and the planks he needed were all ready and waiting. Meanwhile Elisabeth walked along the embankment hedge and gathered little ring-shaped wild-mallow seeds in her pinafore; she would make chains and necklaces with them. When Reinhard had at last finished making the bench, despite several crooked nails, and had come out again into the sun, she was already far away at the other end of the meadow.

'Elisabeth!' he called. 'Elisabeth!' And the little girl came, with her curls flying.

'Come on!' he said, 'our house is finished now. You've got so hot – come inside and we'll sit on the new seat. I'll tell you a story.'

They both went in and sat down on the bench. Elisabeth took the little rings out of her pinafore and started stringing them on long threads, while Reinhard began his story.

‘Once upon a time there were three spinsters…’

‘Oh!’ said Elisabeth, ‘I know that one by heart. You don’t have to tell me the same story every time.’

And so Reinhard had to abandon the story of the three spinsters and tell her instead the tale of the poor man cast into the lions’ den.

‘Then night fell – you know, really dark – and the lions were asleep. But now and then they yawned as they slept, and stretched out their red tongues, and the poor man shuddered and longed for morning to come. Then suddenly a bright light shone all around him, and when he looked up he saw an angel standing before him. The angel beckoned to him with its hand and then disappeared straight into the rock.’

Elisabeth was listening attentively. ‘An angel?’ she said. ‘Did it have wings?’

‘It’s only a story,’ replied Reinhard. ‘There aren’t really any angels.’

‘Oh really, Reinhard!’ she cried, staring him straight in the face, but when he looked sternly back at her she asked, more tentatively, ‘Then why do they all say there are – Mother, Auntie, and the teachers at school too?’

‘I don’t know,’ he replied.

‘Then,’ said Elisabeth, ‘aren’t there any lions either?’

‘Lions? Aren’t there any lions! In India there are – the heathen priests harness them to their carts and drive through the desert! When I grow up I’m going there one day. It’s a thousand times nicer than here. They have no winter at all there! You must come too. Will you?’

‘Yes, but Mother will have to come with us, and your mother too.’

‘No,’ said Reinhard, ‘they’ll be too old by then – they can’t come.’

'But I won't be allowed to come on my own.'

'Of course you will – you'll actually be my wife by then, and no one else will be able to tell you what to do.'

'But my mother will cry.'

'We'll come back again, though. Go on,' said Reinhard impetuously, 'tell me honestly now, do you want to come with me? If not, I'll go alone, and then I'll never come back.'

The little girl was close to tears. 'Don't look so cross,' she said. 'Of course I'll come to India with you.'

Overcome with joy, Reinhard caught her by both hands and dragged her out into the meadow.

'To India! To India!' he sang, and danced her around in a circle till the red kerchief fell from her neck. But then he suddenly let go of her and said in a serious voice, 'But nothing will come of it – you've no courage.'

'Elisabeth! Reinhard!' came a voice from the garden gate.

'We're here!' the children called back, and ran off home, hand in hand.

And so the children lived and grew together. She was often too quiet for him, he too hot-headed for her, but this was not enough to separate them. They spent almost all their spare time together, in their mothers' cramped little rooms in the winter and out in the woods and the fields in the summer.

Once the schoolteacher scolded Elisabeth in Reinhard's presence, and he dashed his slate angrily against the desk, to deflect the teacher's rage onto himself. It went unnoticed. But Reinhard lost all interest in the geography lesson and instead composed a long poem in which he compared himself with a young eagle and the schoolmaster with a grey crow; Elisabeth was a white dove. The eagle solemnly vowed to have his revenge on the crow, just as soon as his wings were big enough. There were tears in the young poet's eyes, and he thought himself quite exalted.

When he came home he found himself a little parchment-bound notebook with many white leaves; on the first page, he wrote out his first poem in a careful hand.

Soon after this he moved to another school. Here he found many new companions among the lads of his own age, but this did not affect his friendship with Elisabeth. Now out of the stories he had told her again and again, he began writing down the ones she had liked best. Often he felt the desire to work in some thoughts of his own, but, without knowing why, he could never quite manage it, and so he wrote down the stories just as he had heard them. Then he gave the pages to Elisabeth, and she put them carefully away in the drawer of her little chest; and it gave him such sweet contentment to sit and listen to her on occasional evenings reading these tales to her mother, out of the notebooks he himself had written.

Seven years had passed. Reinhard was soon to leave the town to continue his education. Elisabeth could not bring herself to accept that a time would come when she would be wholly without Reinhard. She was overjoyed to hear him say one day that he would go on writing stories for her; he would send them to her with his letters to his mother, and she must write back and tell him how she had liked them. His departure was approaching; but many verses still found their way into the little parchment volume. This alone was kept secret from Elisabeth, although she was the inspiration for the book itself and for most of the poems which in the course of time had come to fill almost half its white leaves.

It was June, and Reinhard was to leave the next day. His friends wanted to spend one last day with him, so a large party arranged to go for a picnic to one of the nearby woods. It was an hour's journey to the edge of the forest; they covered the distance by horse and cart, then took their picnic baskets and continued on foot. First they had to cross through a pine forest; here it was cool and shadowy, and the ground was strewn all over with little pine needles. They walked for half an hour, and came out of the darkness of the pine forest into a lush beechwood where all was light and green, and now and then a shaft of sunlight broke through the branches thick with leaves. A squirrel leapt above their heads from branch to branch. At a place where ancient beech trees arched over them, their crowns a translucent dome of leaves, the party came to a halt. Elisabeth's mother opened one of the baskets, and an elderly gentleman put himself in charge of the provisions.

'Gather round, all you young chicks,' he called, 'and listen carefully to what I have to say to you! For your breakfast, each of you will receive two dry bread rolls. We left the butter at home, and you'll have to find the preserves for yourselves. In the woods there are more than enough strawberries – at least for those who know where to find them. If you're not clever enough, then you'll have to eat your bread dry. That's how it is in life; do you understand me!'

'Yes, sir!' cried all the youngsters.

'Wait though!' said the old man. 'I haven't finished yet. We old folk have travelled around quite enough already in our lives – so we'll stay at home now – that is, beneath these wide branches – and peel the potatoes and start a fire and set the table. And on the stroke of twelve we'll boil the eggs. In return for which, you'll owe us half your strawberries, so we can serve a dessert. And now, away with you all, wherever your paths may take you, and behave yourselves!'

The youngsters made all kinds of mischievous faces.

'Stop!' cried the old man once more. 'I know I don't have to tell you this; if you find no berries you won't have to give me any, but mark my words, you won't get anything from us old folk either. And now you've had more than enough good advice for one day; find some strawberries to go with it, and today will pose no problems!'

The youngsters heartily agreed, and in pairs they went on their way.

'Come on, Elisabeth,' said Reinhard, 'I know a good strawberry patch – no dry bread for you!'

Elisabeth tied together the green ribbons of her straw hat and hung it on her arm. 'Come on then,' she said, 'the basket's ready.'

And into the forest they went, deeper and deeper, through damp, impenetrable shadows of trees where all was quiet but for the cry of the falcons hidden in the skies above them, then on through thick brushwood, so thick that Reinhard had to go on ahead to cut a path, breaking a branch here, bending back a tendril there. But soon he heard Elisabeth behind him, calling his name. He turned.

'Reinhard,' she called, 'do wait a moment, Reinhard!' He could not make out where she was, but at last he saw her some way off, struggling with the undergrowth. Her lovely little head hardly rose above the tops of the bracken. He went back again, and led her through the tangled mass of shrubs and bushes out into a clearing where blue butterflies fluttered in and out of the solitary woodland flowers. Reinhard smoothed the moist hair away from Elisabeth's overheated little face; he was about to place the straw hat on her head, but she wouldn't let him. He asked her to wear it, and then she gave way after all.

'So where are your strawberries?' she asked at last, standing still and taking a deep breath.

'They were right here,' he said, 'but the toads got here before us – or the martens, or perhaps it was the elves.'

'Yes,' said Elisabeth, 'the leaves are still here – but please don't talk about elves here. Come on, I'm not at all tired, let's look somewhere else.'

Before them ran a little stream, and on the other side of it the wood stretched on. Reinhard lifted Elisabeth in his arms and carried her over the stream. In a little while they stepped out of the shady foliage into another broad clearing.

'There must be strawberries here,' said the girl, 'there's such a sweet scent.' They walked and searched in this sunny place, but found no berries.

'No,' said Reinhard, 'it is only the smell of the heather.' Thick raspberry bushes and holly grew all around them. The air was filled with the strong fragrance of heather, which covered the ground where the short grass did not grow.

'It's lonely here,' said Elisabeth. 'Where can the others have gone?'

Reinhard had given no thought to the way back. 'Wait a moment, which way is the wind coming from?' he said, and raised his hand in the air – but there was no wind.

'Quiet,' said Elisabeth, 'I think I hear them talking – just shout in that direction.'

Reinhard cupped his hands and called. 'Come over here!'

'Over here!' a call came back.

'They're answering!' said Elisabeth, and clapped her hands.

'No, it was nothing, just the echo.'

Elisabeth clasped Reinhard's hand. 'I'm afraid,' she said.

'No,' said Reinhard, 'you mustn't be afraid; it's wonderful here. Sit down over there in the shade of the bushes. We'll rest awhile; we'll soon find the others all right.'

Elisabeth sat down beneath an overhanging beech and listened attentively in every direction. Reinhard sat a few feet away on a tree stump and gazed at her in silence. The sun shone directly above them with the burning heat of midday; little steel-blue insects hovered in the air, glittering like gold, and all around them was a delicate buzzing and humming; now and again from the depths of the forest they heard the drumming of the woodpecker and the screech of the other woodland birds.

'Listen,' said Elisabeth. 'There's a bell ringing.'

'Where?' asked Reinhard.

'Behind us, can't you hear it? It's midday.'

'Then the town must be behind us, and if we go right on this way we must run into the others.'

And so they started on their way back; they had given up the search for strawberries, for Elisabeth had grown tired. At last there came through the trees the sound of their friends' laughter; then they saw a white cloth lying brightly on the ground. So here was the table, and on it were strawberries in great abundance. The old gentleman had a napkin fastened in his buttonhole, and he was treating the young to more of his moral sermons and at the same time earnestly slicing a joint of meat.

'Ah, the stragglers!' called the youngsters when they saw Reinhard and Elisabeth coming through the trees.

'Over here!' called the old man. 'Empty your handkerchiefs, turn out your hats, and show us what you've found.'

'Nothing but hunger and thirst,' said Reinhard.

'If that is all you have,' replied the old man, lifting up a brimming bowl to them, 'you'll have to keep it for yourselves! You know what we agreed – no food here for lazybones!' But in the end he gave way to their pleading, and in the nearby juniper bushes the thrushes sang their assent as all the party settled down to the feast.

And so the day passed. Reinhard had found something after all; if it was not strawberries, it was still something that had grown in the forest. When he came home again he wrote in his old parchment notebook:

Here on the woodland slope
The wind has grown more mild;
The branches hanging low;
Below them sits the child.

She sits amidst the thyme,
And fragrance fills the air;
The blue flies faintly hum
And sparkle everywhere.

The forest stands so silent,
So wise that child appears
As round her soft brown hair
The sun her charm reveres.

The distant cuckoo laughs,
And now my heart has seen
The lovely golden eyes
Of my own forest queen!

And so she was not only his little charge; she was also the expression of all that was lovely, all that was wonderful at the opening of his life.

Christmas Eve was approaching. It was still afternoon when Reinhard was sitting one day with his fellow-students at an old oak table in the town-hall tavern. The lamps on the walls were lit, as it was already growing dark down there; but there were still only a few customers and the waiters leant idly against the walls. In one corner of the arched cellar sat a fiddler and a zither-girl with fine, gipsy-like features. They had their instruments on their laps, and they seemed to be staring listlessly into the distance.

From the students' table came the pop of a champagne cork. 'Drink, my little Bohemian love!' cried a young man of lordly appearance as he handed a full glass to the girl.

'I don't want to,' she answered, without changing her position.

'In that case sing!' cried the young gentleman, and tossed a silver coin into her lap.

The girl drew her fingers slowly through her black hair while the fiddler whispered something in her ear; she tossed her head and then rested her chin on the zither. 'I'm not playing for him,' she said.

Reinhard leapt up with his glass in his hand and stood right in front of her.

'What do you want?' she asked haughtily.

'I want to see your eyes.'

'And what are my eyes to you?'

Reinhard looked down on her with his own eyes sparkling. 'I know they are false!'

She laid her cheek on the palm of her hand and gave him a searching look. Reinhard raised the glass to his lips. 'Here's to those lovely wicked eyes,' he said, and drank.

She laughed and tossed her head again. 'Give it to me,' she said, and with those dark eyes fixed on his she slowly drained what was left in the glass. Then, striking a chord on the zither, she sang in a deep, passionate voice:

'But this one day
I am so fair;
Tomorrow, ah,
I'll not be there!

But this one hour
You'll be my own;
For when I die,
I'll die alone.'

As the fiddler struck up a lively cadenza a new arrival joined the group.

'I came to collect you, Reinhard,' he said. 'You'd already gone; but the Christ-child had paid you a visit.'

'The Christ-child?' said Reinhard. 'No, he doesn't come to me any more.'

'Nonsense! Your whole room smelt of fir trees and cakes!'

Reinhard put down the glass he was holding, and reached for his cap.

'What are you going to do?' asked the girl.

'I'll be back soon.'

She frowned and said, softly, 'Stay,' and looked at him intimately.

Reinhard hesitated. 'I cannot,' he said.

She laughed and pushed him with the point of her foot. 'Go then,' she said. 'You're worthless. You're all worthless, all of you!' And as she turned from him, Reinhard slowly climbed the cellar stairs.

On the street outside dusk had already closed in, and he felt the chill winter air on his hot brow. Here and there in some of the windows shone the bright lights of Christmas trees, and from time to time there came from inside the sound of toy whistles and tin trumpets, and with them the merry shouts of children. Scores of beggar-children went from house to house, or climbed on the railings and tried to sneak a glimpse of the forbidden splendour through the windows. Now and then a door was suddenly flung open, and scolding voices sent a swarm of these little guests running from the brightness of the house out into the dark lane. In the hallway of another house there was singing – an old Christmas carol sung in the clear voices of little girls. Reinhard heard nothing. He hurried past all this, from one street to another, and when he arrived at his lodging-house it was already almost completely dark. He stumbled up the stairs and into his room. A sweet fragrance greeted him; it reminded him of home, of Christmas at his mother's house. His hand trembling, he lit the lamp, and there before him on the table lay a thick package. He opened it, and out fell the familiar little golden seasonal cakes, some of them bearing his initials iced in sugar. No one but Elisabeth could have done this. Next he found a small bundle of delicately stitched linen cuffs and kerchiefs, and finally letters from his mother and from Elisabeth. It was Elisabeth's letter that he opened first. She wrote:

The pretty little sugar initials will tell you, I think, who helped with the cakes – and it was the same person who stitched the cuffs for you. Christmas is going to be very quiet for us. Mother still puts away her spinning wheel in the corner by half-past nine. It is so lonely here this winter without you. And last Sunday the little linnet you gave me died. I cried a lot, but I know I always looked after him well. He always used to sing in the afternoon when the sun reached his cage. You know, Mother used to hang a cloth over it to quieten him down when he was singing his heart out. So it is now even quieter in the room, except that your old friend Erich occasionally comes visiting. You once said he looked just like his own brown overcoat. Now I can't help thinking about it whenever he comes through the door, and it's so funny. But don't tell Mother, or she'll be angry. What do you think I am going to give your mother for Christmas? You can't guess? Myself! Erich is drawing me in black crayon. I have had to sit for him three times already, a whole hour every time. I didn't like it much at all, a stranger learning my face by heart. I didn't want to go through with it, but Mother talked me into it. She said it would give Mrs Werner such pleasure.

But you don't keep your word, Reinhard. You haven't sent me any stories. I have often complained about you to your mother. She just says that you now have more important things to do than such trifles. But I don't believe it; I think there's some other reason.

Reinhard then read his mother's letter. And when he had read both letters, and slowly folded them and put them away, he was overwhelmed by an irresistible homesickness. For a long time he strode up and down in his room; softly, half-intelligibly he spoke to himself:

'*When he had all but lost his way,*
And knew not where to turn,
A child appeared upon his path;
From her his way he'd learn.'

Then he went to his desk, took some money from it, and returned to the street below. Here in the meantime all had become quieter; the candles on the trees had burnt out, and the children's processions had ended. The wind swept through the lonely streets. Old and young sat together as families in their houses; that second, more private part of Christmas Eve had now begun.

When Reinhard was once again near to the tavern he heard the fiddle-playing and the young zither-girl's singing coming from down below. Then came the sound of the cellar door, and a dark form staggered up the broad, dimly lit stairs. Reinhard retreated into the shadow of the houses and then quickly walked past the tavern. After a little while he reached a brightly lit jeweller's shop, and when he had purchased a small cross made from red coral he started back on the same path he had come by.

Not far from his lodging he noticed a small girl clad in pitiful rags and standing at the large front door of a house. She was trying in vain to open the door.

'Shall I help you?' he said.

The child gave no answer but let go of the heavy door handle. Reinhard had already opened the door.

'No,' he said, 'they might chase you away. Come with me; I'll give you Christmas cakes.' Then he closed the door again and took the little girl by the hand. She accompanied him in silence to his lodging.

He had kept the light burning when he left the building.

'Here are some cakes for you,' he said, and gave her half the entire treasure. He dropped them into her pinafore, but did not give her any of the ones with the sugar letters.

'Now go home, and be sure to give your mother some, too.'

The child looked up at him, timidly. She seemed unused to

such kindness, and lacked the words to respond. He opened the door and lit her way; the little creature flew like a bird down the stairs and out of the house, clutching her cakes.

Reinhard poked the fire in his stove and placed his dust-covered inkstand on the desk. He sat down and wrote. The whole night he sat writing letters to his mother and Elisabeth. The remainder of the cakes lay next to him undisturbed. But he had put on the cuffs that Elisabeth had made, and they looked strange with his shaggy woollen coat. He was still sitting at his desk when the winter sunlight came through the window-panes and revealed to him, in the mirror opposite, a pale, severe countenance.

At Home

When Easter came, Reinhard travelled home. The morning after his arrival, he went see to Elisabeth.

'How you've grown!' he said, when the lovely, slender young girl came smiling towards him. She blushed, but gave no answer. When he took her hand in his to greet her, she gently tried to withdraw it. He looked at her uncertainly; she had never done this before, and now it was as if something strange were coming between them. The impression remained with him even when he had been home for some time and had come day after day to see her. When they sat together alone there were pauses in their conversation, and he found them painful and anxiously attempted to prevent them. So that they might have something particular to do together during the holidays, he began to teach Elisabeth about botany, a subject to which he had occasionally turned his attention during the early months of his life at university. Elisabeth, who had always followed him in everything, and was moreover a very willing pupil, gladly threw herself into her studies.

There now followed, several times each week, excursions into the country and out onto the heath. At noon they returned home with the green plant-box full of specimens of plants and flowers, and a few hours later Reinhard would come back to divide the collection with Elisabeth. It was to this end that he came into the room one afternoon. Elisabeth was standing at the window and decorating a golden birdcage with fresh chickweed. He had not seen the cage before. In it sat a canary, flapping its wings and pecking at Elisabeth's finger and making little screeching sounds. It was in the place where Reinhard's bird had always hung before.

'Has my poor little linnet turned into a goldfinch after

dying?' he asked her cheerily.

'That's not what linnets do,' said Elisabeth's mother, who sat in her armchair spinning. 'Your friend Erich sent him over this morning from the estate.'

'Which estate?'

'Don't you know, then?'

'Know what?'

'That Erich took over his father's second estate at Immensee[1] a month ago.'

'But you never said a word to me about that.'

'Ah,' said the mother, 'but you never uttered a single word of enquiry about your friend. He is a most agreeable, sensible young man.'

The mother went out to prepare coffee. Elisabeth had turned her back to Reinhard and was still busy making the little arbour in the cage. 'Please, just a moment,' she said. 'I'll soon be finished.' As Reinhard, contrary to his usual manner, did not answer, she turned. In his eyes there was a sudden expression of sadness which she had never seen there.

'What is troubling you, Reinhard?' she asked, coming towards him.

'Me?' he asked, blankly, his eyes looking absent-mindedly into hers.

'Yes, you look so unhappy.'

'Elisabeth, I can't stand that yellow bird.'

She looked at him in astonishment. She did not understand him. 'You are so strange,' she said. He took both her hands, and she calmly let them rest in his. Soon her mother came back in.

After the coffee her mother returned to her spinning. Reinhard and Elisabeth went into the adjoining room to work on their plants. Filaments were counted, leaves and petals opened out with meticulous care, and two specimens of each item laid out for drying between the pages of a large folio book. The stillness of the sunny afternoon was broken only by the whirr of the mother's spinning, and from time to time the muffled sound of Reinhard's voice as he named the order and classes of the plants for Elisabeth, or corrected her still inexpert pronunciation of the Latin terms.

'I still don't have a lily of the valley,' she said, when everything that they had collected was identified and put in order.

Reinhard took a little parchment book from his pocket. 'Here's a lily of the valley for you,' he said, taking out a half-dried stem.

Elisabeth saw the writing on the leaves of the book, and asked, 'Have you been writing more stories?'

'They're not stories,' he answered, handing the little volume to her.

The book contained only poems, most of them occupying a page at most. Elisabeth turned over page after page, but she seemed to be reading only the titles of the verses: 'When she was scolded by the teacher', 'When they were lost in the wood', 'A tale for Easter', 'When she first wrote to me'. Almost all of them had titles in that vein. Reinhard looked at her, searchingly, and as she continued to turn the leaves he saw at last a gentle blush appear on her fair cheeks and spread over her face. He wanted to see her eyes, but Elisabeth did not look up, and finally she laid the book down in front of him in silence.

'Don't give it back like that,' he said.

She took a little brown sprig from a tin box. 'I'll put your favourite plant inside it,' she said, and placed the book in his hands.

At last the final day of his vacation came; it was the morning of his departure. At her request, Elisabeth was permitted by her mother to accompany her friend to the stagecoach, which stopped a few streets away from where they lived. When she stepped out of the house Reinhard gave her his arm; and then he walked in silence beside the slim young girl. As they came nearer their destination he felt more and more that he had something of importance to say to her before taking his leave for such a long time – something on which depended all the worth and all the sweetness of his future life; and yet he could not find the words to release him from his burden. It troubled him, and he walked more and more slowly.

'You'll arrive too late,' she said. 'St Mary's has already struck ten.' But this did not make him walk faster.

At last he spoke, falteringly: 'Elisabeth, you will not see me at all now for two whole years – will you be just as fond of me as you are now, when I am back?'

She nodded, and looked tenderly into his eyes. 'I've even defended you,' she said, after a pause.

'Me? And before whom did you have to do that?'

'Before my mother. We spoke about you for a long time last night after you went. She was saying you are not so good now as you were before.'

Reinhard fell silent for a moment. Then he took her hand in his, and looked earnestly into her childlike eyes. 'But I am just as good now as I was – you must believe this. Do you believe it, Elisabeth?'

'Yes,' she said.

He released her hand and passed quickly with her through the last street. The nearer their parting came, the happier his expression grew. He walked almost too quickly for her.

'What is the matter, Reinhard?' she asked.

‘I have a secret, a beautiful secret,’ he said, and looked at her with shining eyes. ‘You will find out about it when I am back again in two years.’

Meanwhile they had reached the coach, with little time to spare. Once again Reinhard took her hand. ‘Goodbye,’ he said. ‘Goodbye, Elisabeth. Don’t forget!’

She shook her head. ‘Goodbye,’ she said. Reinhard climbed in, and the horses pulled off. The coach rounded the street corner, and he caught sight one last time of her beloved form as she slowly started on her way home.

A Letter

Almost two years later Reinhard was sitting by his reading lamp surrounded by books and papers. He was awaiting the arrival of a friend with whom he often shared his study hours. Someone came up the stairs.

'Come in!'

It was his landlady. 'A letter for you, Herr Werner.' And she withdrew.

Since his visit home he had not written to Elisabeth, and he had received no further letter from her. Nor was this one from her; it was his mother's hand. Reinhard broke the seal and read:

At your present stage of life, my dear child, almost every year has its own fresh appearance, for youth will never allow itself to be subdued. Here too, there have been changes which will at first cause you some pain, if I have correctly understood your feelings. Yesterday Erich at last received Elisabeth's consent, having been twice refused in these last three months. She was never quite able to make the decision, but now she has at last done so. She is, after all, still so young. The wedding is to take place soon, and her mother will then be going away with them.

Many years had now passed. One warm spring afternoon a young man with a strong, sunburned face was walking along a shady downhill path through the woods. He looked intently into the distance with his serious dark eyes, as if awaiting at last some change in the monotonous path he trod – but still no change came. At length he saw a cart slowly coming towards him.

'Hello, my good friend,' called the wayfarer to the farmer who approached him. 'Am I on the road for Immensee?'

'Straight ahead,' said the man, touching his cap.

'Is it still far?'

'You're almost there, sir. Half a pipe of tobacco, and you'll be at the lake; the manor is right next to it.'

The farmer drove past, and the young man quickened his pace beneath the trees. After another quarter of an hour the shade of the trees suddenly gave way to clear light on the left. The path now led past a steep incline, out of which rose the tops of century-old oaks. Beyond these, a broad, sunny landscape opened out; far below lay the lake, calm, deep blue, almost wholly surrounded by green sunlit woods except at one place where the trees parted and offered a distant panorama, until this too was cut off by blue hills. Straight opposite, in the midst of the green foliage of the forest, it was as if snow had fallen on the leaves; the orchard trees were in blossom here, and from their midst on the high bank rose the manor house, white and crowned with red tiles. A stork flew up from the chimney and slowly circled above the water.

'Immensee!' cried the wayfarer, and it was almost as if he had reached his journey's end; for he stood motionless and cast his eyes, over the treetops before him, towards the other shore where the mirrored image of the manor floated, swaying gently, on the surface of the lake. Then all of a sudden he started on his way again.

The path continued almost straight down the hill, so that the trees, which had stood below, once more gave shade, but at the same time obscured the view of the lake; now it flashed only intermittently through the gaps in the branches. Presently the path rose again gently, as the wood disappeared to right and left. In its place, thickly leaved vineyards stretched along the way, and on either side stood the blossoming orchard, where swarms of bees buzzed industriously as they went about their tasks. The well-built figure of a man in a brown overcoat approached the traveller. When he had almost reached him, he swung his cap in the air and called out in a cheerful voice: 'Welcome, welcome, brother Reinhard! Welcome to Immensee!'

'God greet you, Erich, thank you for your welcome!' called the other in answer. They reached one another, and shook hands.

'Is it really you?' said Erich, looking closely into the earnest face of his old schoolfriend.

'Most certainly it is, Erich, and this is you – except that you look perhaps a little happier than you were before.'

A joyful smile came over Erich's simple features and made him look happier still. 'Yes, brother Reinhard,' he said, stretching out his hand to him once more. 'But of course since then I've drawn first prize, as you know.' He rubbed his hands together and cried out with pleasure: 'It will be such a surprise! You are a person she cannot be expecting to see, even in a thousand years!'

'A surprise?' asked Reinhard. 'For whom?'

'For Elisabeth.'

'Elisabeth? Do you mean you didn't tell her about my visit?'

'Not a word, brother Reinhard. She has no idea about it, nor does her mother. I wrote to you in complete secrecy, so that their pleasure would be all the greater. You know how I always used to have my little schemes.'

Reinhard became pensive; his breathing seemed to become heavier the nearer he approached the house. On the left side of the path the vineyards gave way to an extensive kitchen garden which stretched almost to the edge of the lake. In the meantime the stork had alighted and was walking solemnly among the vegetable beds.

'Hey!' called Erich, clapping his hands. 'The long-legged Egyptian is stealing my short bean-poles again!' The bird ascended slowly and flew up to the roof of a new building that lay at the end of the kitchen garden, its walls covered over with entangled trellises of peach and apricot branches.

'That is the distillery,' said Erich. 'I only built it two years ago. My late father had all the farm buildings put up, and the house was built by my grandfather. So that's how we progress, little by little.'

As he spoke, they had come to a wide-open place bordered by the rustic farm buildings at the sides and by the manor at the rear. A high garden wall was attached to both wings of the house and behind it could be seen the dark shapes of lines of yews, and here and there the blossoming branches of lilacs hung down into the courtyard. Farm workers, their faces warm from working and bronzed by the sun, passed through the yard and greeted the friends, while Erich issued one or another of them with an instruction or a question about the day's work.

They had now arrived at the house; a high, cool entrance hall received them, and at the end of it they turned left into a somewhat darker passageway. Here Erich opened a door, and they stepped into a spacious garden room, filled from either side with green twilight created by the massed foliage covering the facing windows. Between them were two high, wide-open folding doors which let in the full light of the spring sun and revealed to the eye a garden of circular flower-beds and high, sheer leafy walls broken by a straight and broad walkway, at the end of which could be seen the lake, and beyond it the woods on the opposite side. As the two friends stepped into the room, a sudden waft of fragrance reached them on the breeze.

On a terrace in front of the garden sat a girlish white-clad female figure. She stood, and went towards them as they entered, but she stopped halfway as if rooted to the spot, and stared at the stranger without moving. Whereupon he held out his hand to her.

'Reinhard!' she cried. 'Reinhard! Heavens, it's you! It's so long since we saw each other.'

'Yes, so long,' he said, but could say no more, for when he heard her voice he felt in his heart a sharp burst of pain; and as he looked at her he saw standing before him that same slender, delicate creature to whom he had said farewell so many years ago in the town of his birth.

Erich had stayed behind at the door, his face beaming with pleasure. 'Now, Elisabeth,' he said, 'this is someone you'd surely never have expected, isn't it?'

Elisabeth looked at him with sisterly eyes and said, 'Erich, you are so good!'

He took her delicate hand lovingly in his. 'And now we have him with us, we won't let him go so soon. He has been away so long, we must make him feel at home again. Just see, what a foreign and distinguished look he's acquired!'

Elisabeth glanced shyly at Reinhard's face. 'That's only because of the time we've been apart,' he said.

At this moment her mother came in with a basket of keys on her arm. 'Herr Werner,' she said when she saw Reinhard. 'Well, a guest as welcome as you are unexpected!' And the conversation then took off on a steady course of questions and answers. The women settled down to their work, and while Reinhard enjoyed the refreshment prepared for him, Erich lit his sturdy meerschaum pipe and sat smoking and chatting by his side.

The next day Reinhard was obliged to go out with him into the fields and vineyards and to visit the hop garden and distillery. All of it was well managed; the men who worked the fields and tended the vats all had a healthy, contented look about them. At midday the family gathered in the garden room and the rest of the day was spent more or less in company, depending on how much time the hosts could spare. Reinhard, however, spent the hours before the evening meal, and those in the early morning, working in his room. For years, wherever he had the opportunity, he had been collecting the poems and songs that survived among the ordinary people. His task now was to set this treasury in order and, where possible, expand it with new annotations on this region. Elisabeth was at all times gentle and friendly with him. Erich's constant and devoted attention was accepted by her with almost submissive gratitude, and from time to time the thought occurred to Reinhard that the once lively child had surely promised to be less subdued as a grown woman.

Since the second day of his stay he had been in the habit of taking a walk in the evening on the bank of the lake. The path passed close below the garden, and at its end, on a jutting headland, there was a bench set beneath tall birch trees.

Elisabeth's mother had christened it the 'evening bench', because the place lay to the west and was used most in the evenings to enjoy the sunset. Returning home one evening after a stroll on this path, Reinhard found himself caught in the rain. He sought shelter under a lime tree at the water's edge, but the heavy raindrops soon beat down between the leaves. Soaked through as he was, he resigned himself and set out slowly once more on his way home. It was almost dark. The rain was falling now with ever greater force, and as he approached the evening bench he thought he could discern, between the shimmering birch trunks, a white-clad female form. She stood motionless, and when he came closer it seemed that she was turned towards him, as if waiting for someone. He thought it was Elisabeth. But when he quickened his pace to reach her and accompany her back to the house through the garden, she slowly turned away and disappeared in the dark of the side paths. He could make no sense of it; he felt almost angry with Elisabeth, yet he was still uncertain whether it had been her at all. He hesitated to ask her about it, and on returning he did not enter the garden room, simply to avoid the possibility that he might see Elisabeth coming through the garden gate.

A few days later, when evening was already drawing in, the family sat together in the garden room as they always did at this hour of day. The doors were open; the sun was already down behind the woods on the other side of the lake.

Reinhard was asked to show the others a few of the folk songs he had received that afternoon from a friend who lived in the country. He went up to his room, and presently returned with a paper roll which seemed to consist of single, neatly written sheets.

They sat down at the table, Elisabeth at Reinhard's side.

'Let's just pick some at random,' he said. 'I haven't been through them myself yet.'

Elisabeth unrolled the manuscript. 'There's some music here,' she said. 'You must sing this one, Reinhard.'

And Reinhard first read some Tyrolean hop-picking songs, from time to time half-singing the words to a cheerful melody. A general spirit of merriment came over the little gathering.

'But who composed these lovely songs?' asked Elisabeth.

'Oh,' said Erich, 'you can hear it in the little ditties themselves – tailors, barbers, and all that kind of carefree common rabble!'

Reinhard said, 'They are not composed at all; they grow, they fall from the air, they fly over the land like gossamer, here, there, everywhere, and are sung in a thousand places at once. It is our innermost feelings and sufferings we find in these songs; it is as if we all had a hand in creating them.'

He took up another of the pages: 'I stood upon the mountains high…'

'I know that one,' cried Elisabeth. 'Just sing, Reinhard, and I'll join in.' And now they both sang the melody, so puzzling, so mysterious that one could scarcely believe it was the invention of man at all – she accompanying his tenor voice with her slightly reticent contralto.

The mother sat meanwhile busily sewing. Erich had his hands folded together and listened, thoughtfully. When the song came to an end Reinhard quietly put the sheet to one side. And all of a sudden, up from the shore of the lake there came through the evening calm the ring of the animals' bells. They listened, unconsciously; and then they heard the clear voice of a young boy singing:

'I stood upon the mountains high
And looked down to the valley…'

Reinhard smiled: 'Do you hear? That's how they pass from one mouth to another.'

'You often hear it sung around these parts,' said Elisabeth.

'Yes,' said Erich, 'that's young Kaspar the herdsman; he'll be driving the heifers home.'

They listened for a little while longer until the ring of the bells had faded behind the farm buildings. 'These are primeval sounds,' said Reinhard. 'They slumber on the forest floor; God knows who first discovered them.'

He drew out another sheet. It had now grown darker; a red glow of evening lay like a misty covering on the woods over the lake. Reinhard unrolled the page, and Elisabeth, putting her hand on one side of it, looked and read with him. Then Reinhard began:

'My mother's wish it was I take
Another man, and thee forsake.
What once I thought was mine,

My heart must now decline,
Though it therewith may break.

My mother, her I now accuse –
How could she thus her daughter use?
What had been honoured gain
Has turned to bitter pain,
As all my hopes I lose.

And all my joy and pride,
By pain are now belied.
Ah! had it not been so,
Then begging I could go
Upon the green hillside!'

During the reading Reinhard had sensed a barely perceptible trembling in the paper. When he finished, Elisabeth gently pushed back her chair and walked in silence down into the garden. Her mother's glance followed her. Erich was about to go out after her, but her mother stopped him: 'Elisabeth has things to do out there.' And that was the end of the matter.

Outside, the evening gradually settled and thickened over garden and lake, and the night moths whirred and darted past the open door, through which the scent of the flowers and shrubs now entered with ever greater intensity. From the water rose the croaking of the frogs. A nightingale started singing beneath the window, and another, deeper down in the garden. The moon looked over the trees. Reinhard continued to gaze for a little while over at the place where Elisabeth's slight figure had vanished among the leafy paths; then he rolled up his manuscript, bade the assembled company goodnight, and went through the house and down to the water's edge.

The woods stood in silence and cast their darkness out over the lake; but the middle of the water still lay in the sultry moonlight. Now and then gentle breezes rustled through the trees; but this was not wind, rather the breath of the summer night. Reinhard continued on his way along the bank. Just a stone's throw from the shore he could make out the shape of a white water lily. All at once the desire seized him to see it from closer by; he threw off his clothes and stepped into the water. It was shallow, and his feet were cut by the stones and plants; he could not find a place where it was deep enough to swim. Then suddenly the bed of the lake fell away. The water swirled over him, and it was some time before he came to the surface again. Now he worked with hands and feet, swimming around in a circle until he once more became conscious of where he had entered the lake. Presently he saw the lily again; it lay alone among the broad, shiny leaves. He swam out slowly, raising his arms from the water from time to time, letting the droplets sparkle in the moonlight. Yet it was as if the distance between him and the flower remained unchanged, except that the bank, when he looked round, was in deeper and deeper haze. But he did not give up; he swam boldly on in the same direction. In the end he had come so close to the flower that he could distinguish the silvery leaves clearly in the moonlight. But at that moment he felt suddenly as if he were entangled in a net; the slippery tendrils of the plants reached up and twined themselves around his naked limbs. The unfamiliar waters around him were so dark, and behind him he heard a fish jump. Everything was now suddenly so uncanny in this strange element; forcefully he freed himself from the mesh of the plants, and with breathless haste made for the shore. When he looked back at the lake the lily was, as before, far away and solitary out in the dark depths. He put on his clothes and went slowly back to the house. Entering the room from the garden, he found Erich and the mother in the midst of preparations for a business trip which they were to make the next day.

'And where have *you* been so late at night?' the mother challenged him.

'I?' he answered. 'I was trying to visit a water lily, but nothing came of it.'

'There you go again, doing such strange things!' said Erich. 'And what the devil did you want with the water lily?'

'I knew her once upon a time,' said Reinhard. 'But that was long ago.'

The following afternoon Reinhard and Elisabeth were walking together on the other side of the lake, now among the trees and now on the high jutting edge of the bank. Elisabeth had received her instructions from Erich; while he and her mother were away, she should acquaint Reinhard with the most beautiful views in the immediate neighbourhood – namely the views of the estate from the other side of the lake. They were now walking from one point to another, and at last Elisabeth became tired and sat down in the shade of the overhanging branches. Reinhard stood opposite her, leaning against a tree. At that moment he heard the call of a cuckoo deep in the wood, and the thought came suddenly that all of this had happened once before. With a strange smile he asked Elisabeth, 'Shall we go and look for strawberries?'

'It's not the season for strawberries,' she said.

'But it soon will be.'

Elisabeth shook her head and said nothing, then stood up. Both continued on their way, and as she walked at his side his eyes repeatedly glanced back at her; she walked so beautifully, as if the very clothes she wore were carrying her. Often he lingered unconsciously a step behind her, just to be able to feast his eyes on her. And so they came to an open place overgrown with heather, which gave them a view that stretched far over the landscape. Reinhard bent down and plucked something from among the plants that grew at their feet. When he looked up again, his face bore an expression of profound inner suffering. 'Do you know this flower?' he said.

She looked at him, questioningly. 'It is an Erica; I've often picked them in the woods.'

'I have an old book at home,' he said; 'I once used to write all kinds of songs and poems in it, but it's a long time since I did that. There is an Erica there too, between the pages, but only an old, withered one. Do you know who gave it to me?'

She nodded mutely, but lowered her eyes and looked at the plant he held in his hand. And they stood there for a long while. When she raised her eyes to him again, he saw that they were full of tears.

'Elisabeth,' he said, 'behind those blue mountains lies our youth. What has become of it?'

They spoke no more, but walked together in silence down to the lake. The air was sultry; to the west, dark clouds were gathering.

'There's going to be a storm,' said Elisabeth, quickening her steps. Reinhard nodded without answering, and the two went quickly along the shore until they reached their boat.

While they crossed the lake Elisabeth rested her hand on the edge of the boat. As he rowed, Reinhard looked over towards her, but she stared past him into the distance. So his eyes fell and rested on her hand, and that pale hand betrayed to him everything that her face had hidden. In it he saw the subtle hints of private pain, the pain which so often leaves its signs on a woman's beautiful hands that lie at night folded over a stricken heart. When Elisabeth felt his eyes resting on her hand, she slowly let it slip over the side into the water.

Arriving at the estate, they came upon a scissor-grinder's cart standing before the manor house. A man with long black curls was busy turning the wheel while humming a gipsy melody between his teeth; a panting dog lay tied up close by. A girl stood at the entrance to the house. She was dressed in rags, and bore the signs of a beauty now lost. She stretched out a begging hand to Elisabeth.

Reinhard reached into his pocket, but Elisabeth anticipated

him and hastily poured the entire contents of her purse into the beggar-girl's open hand. Then she turned hurriedly away, and Reinhard heard her sobbing as she went up the steps. At first he thought to hold her back, but then thought better of it, and lingered on the steps himself. The girl was still in the vestibule, motionless, holding in her hand the alms she had received.

'What else do you want?' asked Reinhard.

She started back in fright. 'Nothing more,' she said, and with her head turned towards him and staring at him with confusion in her eyes she went slowly to the door. He called out a name, but she no longer heard him; with head bowed low, her arms crossed over her breast, she passed over the yard.

For when I die
I'll die alone.

An old song rang in his ears, and his breath went still within him. A little time passed, and then he turned back and went up to his room.

He sat down to work, but no ideas came to him. After trying in vain for a whole hour he went down to the family room. There was no one there, only the cool, green twilight. On Elisabeth's sewing table lay a red ribbon which she had been wearing around her neck that afternoon. He picked it up, but it pained him, and he put it down again. He could not rest, and went down to the lake and untied the boat; he rowed to the other side and revisited all the paths that he had walked with Elisabeth just a short while before. When he returned to the house it was dark. In the yard he met the coachman, who was about to take the horses out to pasture; the travellers had just returned.

On entering the hall, he heard Erich pacing up and down in the garden room. He did not go in to join him, but stood silently for a moment and then went quietly back up the stairs to his room. Here he sat down in the armchair at the window, and pretended to himself that he wanted to hear the sound of the nightingale singing in the yew trees below. But all that he could hear was the sound of his own heart. Downstairs all was silent in the house; the night was quickly passing, but he did not sense it. And thus he sat for hours. Finally he rose, and leant forward through the open window. The night dew drizzled among the leaves; the sound of the nightingale had ceased. Gradually, the deep blue of the night sky was giving way to a pale yellow glow from the east. A fresh breeze rose and brushed against Reinhard's fevered forehead. The first lark soared jubilantly into the air. Reinhard suddenly turned round. He went to the table and felt around for a pencil. When he had found one, he sat and wrote a few lines on a sheet of white paper. When he had finished writing, he took his hat and stick. Leaving the paper on the table, he cautiously opened the door and went down to the hall. The half-light of early morning still pervaded every corner. The large house-cat lay stretched on the straw mat; it arched its back against the hand he held out absently. But outside in the garden the sparrows were already holding forth from the branches, telling all the world that night was over. At that moment he heard a door open in the house. Someone was coming down the stairs; when he looked up, Elisabeth was standing before him. She laid her hand on his arm and her lips moved, but he heard nothing. At last she said, 'You will never come back. I know it, do not lie to me; you will never come back.'

'Never,' he said. She let her hand fall, and said no more. He crossed over the hall to the door; then once more he turned.

She stood, motionless, in the same place and looked at him with lifeless eyes. He took one step forward and stretched out his arms towards her. Then, controlling himself, he turned away and went through the door. Outside lay the world in the fresh light of morning. The dewdrops, hanging in the spiders' webs, glistened in the first rays of sun. He did not look back, but hastily made his way out. Behind him the estate, in its stillness, sank further and further from view, while before him rose the great, wide world.

The moon now shone no longer through the window-panes; all had grown dark, but still the old man sat in the armchair, hands folded, and stared in front of him into the empty space of his room. By degrees, the dark twilight dissolved before his eyes into a wide, black lake. One dark mass of water appeared behind another, receding ever deeper and more remote; and upon the very last, so far away that the old man's eyes could scarcely reach it, there swam, solitary among broad green leaves, a white water lily.

The door of the room opened, and a bright stream of light entered. 'It's good that you've come, Brigitte,' said the old man. 'Just put the lamp on the table.'

And then he pushed the chair up to the table, took one of the books that lay open on it, and immersed himself in studies that once had engaged the energies of his youth.

A Quiet Musician

Ah, the old music master! Christian Valentin was his name. Sometimes, as dusk is falling and I sit dreaming in front of my warm stove, his gaunt form floats into my mind, clad in that threadbare, black coat of his. And then, when he gradually fades from my vision – just like all the other visitations I receive, in silence and unobserved – and recedes into the thick haze from which he rose to view just a moment before, there is always a trembling somewhere in my heart, as if I wanted to stretch out my arms to him, and hold him, and send him on his solitary journey with some comforting word of affection.

The two of us had lived close to each other for several years in a town in northern Germany; the little man with thinning, fair hair and pale blue eyes had passed by me, often seen but just as often unnoticed, until one day I found myself together with him in an antiquarian bookshop. This was the beginning of our acquaintance; we were both of us collectors, each in his own way. On entering the shop I had noticed a copy of Hauff's *Lichtenstein*[1] in his hand, and I could see that he was engrossed in the book as he leant against the counter.

'That's a delightful book you have there,' I said, rather by way of reply to the greeting he had given me despite his absorbed reading of the pages.

He looked at me. 'Yes, indeed!' he said, and his pale eyes lit up and an honest, childlike smile brightened his otherwise somewhat plain features. 'Are you fond of it, too? I'm so glad; I find I can read it over and over again.'

We now started to converse, and I told him how the year before I had visited the place where the work was written and had seen, to my great pleasure, a bust of the author on a rock ledge near to the castle he had so immortalised. He seemed quite unsatisfied by this.

'Only a bust?' he said, 'For such a man they could surely

have erected a whole statue!… You're laughing at me,' he added immediately, with the same diffident but affable manner. 'It's true, my taste may not be of the highest order.'

I came to know him better after this. His taste was in fact far from common, but just as in music he was content with his Haydn and his Mozart, so in poetry it was the lucid spring songs of Uhland, or the tranquil poems of Hölty that I used to see lying open on his table.[2]

Whenever we met after this at the bookshop, or even just on the street, we fell into the habit of walking a little way and chatting together; I learnt that he lived and worked here in the town of his birth as a piano teacher, though he gave lessons only in the homes of the middle-class citizens or in families of the less well-off civil servants. He made no secret of the fact that his earnings were sufficient only for a modest lodging, which he had occupied for some years now, in the house of a bleacher who lived close to the town.

'Ah, well,' he said, 'it's good enough for an old bachelor; one shouldn't have any silly notions above one's station! I look out of my window, when it isn't covered over with washing, onto the beautiful green bleaching field. I used to play there when I was a boy, and helped our maidservants carry the heavy linen-baskets out there. The apple tree, which was shaken for me so often, is still there, just where it used to be.'

And, to be sure, I did not find his little room so bad at all when one afternoon, after a walk in his company, I went in with him. The field was at this time free of washing, and it radiated a green lustre through the window. On the wall above the sofa hung two of the better-known woodland studies by Lessing[3] – from his father's estate, he told me. Over the well-maintained piano, which he kept with its lid open, hung an exquisite chalk drawing of a female head, surrounded by a green wreath. As I stood and contemplated this portrait, he came up to me and began somewhat timidly: 'I have to tell you, for you would otherwise find it hard to believe, that this noble face once belonged to my dear mother – yes, really!'

'I can well believe it!' I answered, for his face was right before me, transformed, as I had so often seen it, by affection and friendship.

And as if he had guessed my thoughts, he added: 'You should have seen her smile; there's no life in the picture.'

When later we came to talk about his favourite composers, every now and then he would play a few bars on the piano from some movement or other, by way of illustrating what he said. But whenever I begged him to play on he became almost embarrassed, and attempted to evade my request. Finally, when I pressed him more forcefully, he said, with some anxiety, 'No, please do not ask this of me; it is many years since I played.'

'But look at this,' I replied, and pointed to a score of the *Four Seasons* lying open on the piano music stand. 'Surely none of your pupils can be playing this?'

He nodded eagerly. 'You're right. But I'm just reading it. It's vital to have something like that to do if you're constantly giving elementary instruction. It's a tremendous achievement for one man to have written all that.' And he turned the pages of the large volume enthusiastically back and forward.

After a little while I left, and on my way out I saw fastened to the door a small slip of paper, on which a somewhat angular hand had written a few bars from a Mozart '*Ave Verum*'. On other later visits I noticed that the paper was replaced from time to time, either with the sayings of some writer or, more often, a few bars from a classical composition. Once I asked him about this peculiarity, and again I saw that childlike smile shining in his face. 'It's a fine greeting, don't you think?' he said, with genuine feeling, 'when you come back tired to your little home!'

And thus we saw something of each other for a good length of time without my learning any more significant details about him, until one autumn evening when, by the glow of a street lamp which had just been lit, I saw him coming out of the gateway of a large house. As I had no plans other than to refresh myself with a little stroll up and down the street after an exacting day's work, I called out to him. He nodded warmly when he recognised me.

'And since when, my dear friend,' I asked, 'have you been giving tuition at the houses of the patrician classes?'

He laughed. 'Me? You're making fun of me! No, it's the young scholar from Leipzig who is having lessons. You must surely know him – a superlative musician. He played to me just now for over an hour. I can assure you, he's a wonderful young man.'

'Do you really know him that well?' I asked, with a smile.

'No, I suppose I don't know him very well, but a musician of that quality must also be a good person!'

I could find no reason to disagree.

'Do you have time for a little stroll with me?' I asked. He nodded, and we set off together down the street.

'I've just given my last lesson,' he said, 'to the daughter of a schoolteacher who lives over there on the square. She's another one with a heart of gold, and a real talent for music, too.'

'But don't you have the children come to your house? It's not so far from here.'

He laughed and shook his head. 'No, no, I couldn't demand that! But she, yes, it's true, she does come to see me at my lodgings. It's just that she has recently recovered from a serious illness. She's already starting to tackle Mozart. And what a voice she has! Still, for the moment it's too early for that; she's only thirteen.'

'So you give singing lessons too?' I asked. 'You must be the only one around here with any expertise in that field.'

'Good heavens! Nothing of the sort!' he answered. 'No, it's only that in her case, since any one of the real teachers is beyond the reach of a schoolmaster's daughter, I felt I'd like to have a try myself, with God's help. Once in the past I lived under the same roof as an old lady singer. She had had something of a name in Mozart's day; indeed, it was really thanks to the great man himself that she sang at all. I have to admit that her poor old throat was by then little better than a door hinge! In fact,' he added more discreetly, 'a mischievous young girl, the daughter of the man who was then my landlord, once even suggested it was like the voice of our music-loving pet cat, and she gave the good lady the nickname "Signora Caterina". But Signora Caterina certainly knew all about singing. The two of us went through a fair number of appalling duets together. She could never have enough of this. But what I gained from it, by and by, was nothing less than the knowledge of an entire singing method. "Please pay careful attention, Monsieur Valentin," she used to say, as she raised herself on tiptoe and with the fingertips of one hand took hold of her cap, which I must say was never exactly clean at the best of times. "This is how the great Maestro intended it!" And then, from her old, parched throat there would fly, with rare confidence and quite surprising stresses, a coloratura to some Mozart aria. If in her opinion I'd done a good job, she used to produce from her handbag a crystal sweetmeat box, always full, and pop a peppermint pastille into my mouth with her own withered old fingers. God bless her, my dear old friend!' he said, with sudden gentleness in his voice. 'Who knows, perhaps a young person could still derive some profit from these last exertions of an old lady. For' – and here he tapped his forehead with his fingers – 'up here I have safely stored what the immortal master wanted from the young prima donna's singing.'

To break the silence into which my friend now fell, I began, 'You have never spoken to me of your early days. Was there much music at home in your parents' house?'

'Certainly,' he answered. 'Why else would I have become a musician?'

'Was that the only reason, my friend? I can hardly believe that.'

'Well, I suppose it may also have been my true calling. But I was always severely held back by a certain weakness in the head. Oh, you have no idea how severely! The first time I heard the organ played in a village church I broke into sobs and couldn't be quieted. But it wasn't the power of the music that did this to me; even the sudden sound of a doorbell near me had exactly the same effect. No, it was this poor, weak head that I carried on my shoulders since childhood.' He remained standing for a moment, then I heard him sigh, as if wrestling with some personal grief.

'My father,' he continued, after a short while, 'knew nothing about such things. He was a down-to-earth type, a well-regarded and very busy lawyer here in town. I lost my dear mother when I was just in my twelfth year, and after that I lived alone with him; my brothers and sisters were older, and had all already left home. Apart from his legal papers and a special collection of history books, which I lacked the intellect to use properly despite all his encouragement to do so, he had only one real hobby, and that was music. To tell the truth, it was from him that I received my essential tuition. Probably it would have been better if I had had it from someone else. Please do not misunderstand me; I remember, and am deeply grateful for, the affectionate trouble he took, but when my debility overcame me he easily became impatient, impetuous, and this only served to confuse me utterly. I suffered at that time a good deal through my condition. I see clearly now that there was nothing he could do to help; with his quick mind he was unable to understand what was happening to me; all he could see was an innate indolence which just needed to be shaken out of me. But one day – it was when I was about to have my confirmation – he did, for all that, come to understand. Oh, dear father, I shall never forget that day!'

Stretching out his arms and letting them fall again, he continued: 'We were sitting together at the piano in the living-room and playing a four-hand sonata by Clementi. The night before, I had been sitting up late over a difficult chapter in my harmony book, and I had woken up that day with what my dear departed mother used to call a 'light' head. We were in the middle of the rondo, and my thoughts became muddled, I made a whole succession of mistakes, and my father shouted, "How can you do this! You've played the piece twenty times!" He turned back the pages of the score and we started the movement again. But it was no good – I could not get through the fatal passage. He leapt up and hurled back his chair. I don't know what happens in other families, but for all my father's quick temper I had never suffered a single blow from him. There was very likely something else weighing on his mind; now, when I was almost out of my childhood, he fell prey to his temper.

'The score had fallen from the music stand onto the floor. Silently I picked it up. My cheeks burned. My breast swelled as if blood would rush from my mouth. But I settled myself again and put my trembling hands on the keys. My father, too, sat beside me, and with not a word, nor a glance passing between us we pressed on with the sonata. Even now I cannot say, though I have often asked myself, whether perhaps the enormous pain I felt had wondrously enlivened my powers for a moment – but all of a sudden I found it easy, the printed marks in the score seemed to transform themselves into notes, as if there were between them no longer any black and white keys for my clumsy fingers to negotiate.

'"You see?" said my father, "you can do it when you want to!"

'The sonata was over. Since things had gone so unusually well, he immediately put another piece in front of me on the piano. I was to play this one as a solo. I started off quite confidently, but as my father was not playing with me, but standing at my side and watching keenly, I became confused and struggled in vain to retain my sudden new-found security. It is even possible that this bitter charm could work no more anyway. My head swam as if in a mist, my former fear gripped me, and away went my thoughts like birds on the wing and vanished, far off in the grey sky.

'I stopped playing. "Don't hit me, Father," I cried, and pushed against his chest with both hands. "There's something wrong with me; it's my head. I can't do anything about it!"

'When I looked up at him like this, my father was staring at me intently. I was probably deathly pale; there was little colour to me even at the best of times.

'"Play it again, for yourself," he said calmly. Then he left me and I heard him go up the stairs towards his room.

'I could not play. I was overwhelmed by a despair I had never known, and in self-pity I felt my soul itself would be carried off. Over the piano hung a portrait of my mother, the one you recently saw in my lodgings. I can still see myself stretching out my hands and repeating over and over in childish incomprehension the same words: "Help me, Mother, please help me!" Then I put my head in my hands and wept bitterly.

'How long I sat like this, I cannot say. I had already heard movement outside in the hall, but I had not stirred, although I knew that there was no one other than myself on this side of the house. Finally there was a knock from outside; I got up and opened the door. It was a workman I knew, wanting to talk to my father about some business matter. "Are you ill, young sir?" asked the man. I shook my head and said, "I'll see if it's convenient."

'When I entered my father's room he was standing next to one of his huge book shelves. I had often seen him in this position, pulling out some volume or other, turning its pages and then replacing it on the shelf. Today, however, was different. He was leaning with his arm against the edge of one of the shelves, and he had covered his eyes with his hand.

'"Father!" I said softly.

'"What is it, child?"

'"There is someone who wishes to speak to you."

'He did not answer me; he took his hand from his eyes, and gently called my name. Then I lay against my father's breast, for the first time in my life. I sensed that he wanted to speak, but he only stroked my hair and looked at me, pleadingly. "My poor, dear boy!" These were the only words that he managed to utter. I closed my eyes; I felt protected from all life's troubles. In spite of my mother's death I kept forgetting that everything dies and everything changes.

'But from that moment on it was a happy time for me at home. My father was never once short-tempered with me again; a mother could not have treated me more gently than he did. And the spring came in those days with a beauty I can scarcely recall from any time since. Behind the town, between hedgerows and embankments, was a deserted place where a summer-house had once stood, but which now seemed completely abandoned. Among the flowers that must once have grown there, the only ones now to be found were the violets, which bloomed in the first days of spring. I went there often; and later too, when the hawthorn in the hedgerows was covered with snow-white flowers or when all the blossom was gone and only the little linnets and yellowhammers darted in and out of the bushes. Many an hour I spent there lying in the grass; it was so quiet and mysterious – the only voices were those of the leaves and the birds. But I never saw the place clothed in such beauty as I did that spring. Like me, the bees had already gone out into the meadow, and now they wove and hummed in and out of the myriad violet flowers which burst open in a blue lustre from grass and moss. I gathered them and filled my pocket handkerchief; it was as if I was enchanted, in the midst of the fragrance and sunlight. Then I sat down in the grass, took out some thread which I always carried with me, and began, like a girl, to make a garland. Above me in the clear sky a lark was singing with all its heart; "O, thou divine and lovely world!" I thought. And so I found myself composing verse. Of course my efforts were no more than childish thoughts in the conventional rhymes, but they brought me the greatest joy and satisfaction.

'When I came home I hung the chain of violets in my father's study. I remember it still, the happiness I felt in being able now to indulge in such trifles with him.

'But there is something else. Later, in his legacy to me, I found a savings book in my name, containing a considerable sum. The first deposit, clearly shown by the date, had been made by him on that same bitter-sweet day. I was much affected by the discovery of this book together with his will. Fortunately I had no need of his support.'

We had just emerged from the remote backstreets that our steps had taken us along involuntarily as we conversed; we now turned into one of the main streets. While I was almost furtively watching the ageing man at my side, he suddenly put his hand on my arm.

'Would you like to have a look?' he said. 'This is where we lived when my parents were alive. We owned the house, but after my father's death it had to be sold.'

I looked up, and saw the row of windows on the upper storey brightly lit.

'I could have had some very good lessons here once,' he began again, 'but I couldn't bring myself to accept; I was afraid I might meet a poor, pale youngster on the stairs – a man who hadn't come to much.' He fell silent.

'Do not say such things!' I said. 'I thought till now you were just as happy as the rest of us.'

'Yes, of course!' he replied quietly, slightly embarrassed, and adjusted his grey felt hat a few times. 'I am, indeed I am! It was just a sudden fancy. Normally I know one shouldn't allow oneself these silly notions.'

I had noticed some time ago that this last phrase served him as a defence, a means of closing the door on all vain hopes and desires.

A quarter of an hour later we were in my room, where I had invited him to share my evening meal. While I was busy brewing a pot of northern punch over my spirit stove, he stood at my book shelf surveying, with obvious delight, the attractive row of Chodowiecki[4] books.

'But you are missing one,' he said. 'The poems of Bürger[5], with the long list of subscribers. I find it's such a pleasure looking for one's own forebears among all the other notables. I'm sure you'd also find some of yours.' He looked at me with his warm smile. 'I happen to have a spare copy; would you care to come by some time and pick it up?'

I accepted his offer gratefully. And soon we were sitting next to each other on the sofa, the steaming glasses before us; he was smoking my longest pipe, which he had asked for in preference to the cigars I offered. When he had tasted the punch, he held the glass in his hand and said, nodding at it, 'We always used to drink this at home on New Year's Eve. Once when I was a boy I became quite drunk on it and for years I felt an aversion to this noble concoction. But now – well, now I like it again!' He took a contented draught and placed his glass on the table.

We smoked and chatted, and the conversation led us here and there, from subject to subject. 'No,' he said, 'in those days in our country we didn't have what we now call Conservatoires. I was placed in the hands of a competent piano master and I worked conscientiously for a few years at my theory and technique. There was one other student apart from me, and it wasn't long before he rejoiced in the title "court pianist". And yet, when I sat from time to time and listened to his playing, I could not help thinking that I, Christian Valentin, could do all this much better, if only my fingers and thoughts had worked more efficiently together. You see,' he added, as he laid his thumb and little finger in a wide span on the tablecloth, 'you see, this is not the problem: these are a real keyboard-player's hands.'

'Perhaps,' I interrupted, 'you were too severe on yourself; in players of less refined talents, nothing stands between the thoughts and the fingers!'

He shook his head. 'No, it's not that. And even if I were... No, I simply cannot control it. Before I settled down here permanently, I lived for some time as a music teacher in another town. There were no demands on me to give concert performances, and I dare say I did manage to achieve something there. What is more, although the tuition fees were only modest, I managed in those first years to put aside a small amount for the future – whether for solitary old age as a bachelor, or perhaps...'

He took up his glass and drained it at one go. 'There!' he cried. 'That's given me strength! I'm happy to tell you all about it; I even feel I could play you my Mozart again now!'

He had taken both my hands in his. There was a light flush on his pale cheeks. 'At that time I lived in the house of a master bookbinder,' he began again. 'He ran an antiquarian bookshop next door. Many a fine little volume found its way into my collection in those days! One who made fun of me for stumbling up to my room with tattered little volumes, as if they were the most priceless plunder, was my bookseller's daughter. She had a pretty name – Anna. She had little time for books, but made up for this with her singing – folk songs and operatic arias. God knows where her young ears had picked it all up. And what a voice she had! Signora Caterina, who occupied an attic room in the same house, was in a constant state of indignation that this "silly child", as she called her, would not allow her to teach her. "Monsieur Valentin," she cried once, as Anna stood laughing before her after a long scolding, "look at this child! She has this good fortune in her very house, and all she can do is kick it away with her little feet, and then… Oh, little children! Well, old age creeps up on you unawares! As I stand here before you, I could have married princes and Excellencies!"

'"And I," said the silly child, "can still marry a prince – and that's what I'm going to do, just as soon as he rides up in his golden coach! But Signora, can *you* do *this*?" And she sang, with the most astounding fluency, one of those rhymes made up of tongue-twisting nonsense syllables – forwards, backwards, up and down they went. "You see, Signora, that's natural talent!"

'The old opera singer would not usually deign to answer such wanton cheek, and this time too she silently wrapped herself in the red shawl she never let fall from her shoulders even indoors, and ascended, her head raised in dignity, to her little attic room.

'When she had gone, little Anna put her hands behind her back, and standing in front of me like a bird on a branch, began to sing again. "Swabian maid, hurrah! Bavarian maid, hurrah!" And the "hurrah" soared like a fireball in the air. Then she looked at me with her brown eyes and asked, guilelessly, "That really is beautiful, isn't it, Herr Valentin?"

'We were in my room one evening; Anna had as usual brought me my meal. I sat down at the piano. "Sing some more, Anna," I said, and she sang the song through to the end, while I played a simple accompaniment. Then came another song, and a third, and I couldn't say how many more of her pretty little ditties. All I know is that I was unutterably happy.

'"No!" cried the lovely child, "how is that possible? Do you know *all* my songs? But you know something, Herr Valentin, the whole house must have been ringing with them. Signora Caterina must be sitting up there completely covered in her shawl!"

'From that day, little Anna thought I must be capable of achieving anything in music! Indeed, I myself was gradually beguiled by this naive admiration and I derived much confidence from it. On one occasion, just after she left me, I even sat down and eagerly reckoned up my abilities and resources. I can tell you quite simply, that girl, the "silly child", had come to influence every thought of mine. But then – then the *Liedertafeln*[6] came into fashion.'

'The *Liedertafeln*?' I asked, puzzled, but used the pause in our conversation to fill my friend's glass from the invigorating brew which stood steaming in a pot in front of us over the little blue flame.

'Yes, alas, the *Liedertafeln*,' he repeated, and he drew forcefully on his pipe, emitting large smoke-rings in front of him. 'I never felt comfortable with them – those never-ending male voices. It was as if I would be playing only in the lower octaves year in, year out. And what's more, the odours of the beer tavern quickly became inseparable from them. Still, I was unable to resist accepting the post I was offered as director of the new local *Liedertafel*. A motley crew they were: artisans, tradesmen, civil servants. We even took on a nightwatchman – an ordinary enough fellow, but he had an extraordinary bass voice. And no harm in that; art seems to me such a sublime pursuit that there is no room for mundane discriminations.

'I must tell you that in those days we used to practise with enormous seriousness and enthusiasm; when one voice went through his part there was certainly no idle chatter among the other singers; they had their noses in their scores, mentally fitting their parts to what they were hearing. Anyway, we soon had two of our winter concerts successfully behind us, and the third was approaching. A few days before it was to take place, our principal tenor fell ill. He was a rare bird indeed, with a prodigious high B flat! Without him, several of the numbers we had prepared so painstakingly became quite unworkable.

'I went around pondering how we could possibly fill the gaps in the programme. But little Anna had really decided the question for me long in advance: "Get them to take your piano into the hall, and play something yourself. Why waste your lovely music the whole time on a silly little creature like me, and that ageing artiste upstairs?"

'I wagged my finger to start with, but she got her way. I chose the Mozart *Fantasy-Sonata* for the recital; this was before the piece had become a favourite for all pupils to churn out on every occasion. Morning and evening, before and after my lessons, I sat and practised keenly. And when I immersed myself in the piece I felt from time to time that the Master himself nodded approvingly. I heard his voice clearly, saying to me, "That's right, absolutely right, dear Valentin! That is precisely what I had in mind!" One time, just as I had come to the end of the adagio, I suddenly became aware of Signora Caterina standing at the open door of my room, emitting a brittle laugh in that broken soprano voice of hers – something I was finding quite detestable at the time. She maintained, still laughing, that I had spoken these words of encouragement myself, quite audibly and with great reverence! Then she patted my cheeks with her thin, heavily ringed hand: "Now, now, *caro amico*[7],' she said, "the great Maestro is no longer there in person, but his disciple is here, and she cries 'bravo, bravissimo!' Now let's have it da capo[8], and we'll really have something to listen to!"

'And while I repeated the adagio, she stood behind my chair offering little comments through words and gestures. You cannot believe what fine musicianship still lingered on in this old soul, yet when the frenzy of singing came over her in the presence of others almost everyone had trouble choking back the laughter. I alone never experienced this; the effect she was still able to produce, with her formidable gifts, overwhelmed me – it was not pity I felt, for she was in no need of that, but rather an unaccountable sense of awe, almost as if it were I that had surrendered myself, not she. Of course she sensed nothing of this; proud as a queen, draping herself in her red cashmere shawl, she took up her position in the middle of the room, and sounded forth her great arias. I have to confess that when the two of us were alone together, in my passionate desire to learn, it was more her soul than her voice I heard sing. For what she desired to express, and what I felt I could hear before long, was almost always right.

'And so on this occasion too I sat at the piano on the eve of my concert, as her obedient and attentive pupil. I was hardly troubled by the familiar sound of little steps coming up the stairs. Indeed I scarcely even saw the stern gesture with which the signora dismissed little Anna as she came softly in. But, as if under a compulsion, she came gradually closer, and soon, with her arms tucked in her pinafore, she leant on the piano beside me and I felt her large, brown eyes watching me steadily. I played on, utterly inspired. When I came to the end, little Anna heaved a deep sigh. "That was beautiful!" she said. "Heavens, Herr Valentin, the things you can play!" The signora laid her ringed hand on my head, as if in an act of blessing. "My dear friend, you will be a great success!" And at that moment I felt a peppermint pastille between my teeth.

'This was all very well. An innocent child, who took pleasure in admiration, and the old musical soul who helped me study – and there was also little Anna's spaniel, little black-spotted Polly; I now noticed that she too had been sitting in the doorway, quiet as a mouse. Yes, that was the kind of audience I could do with! But later in front of all those strangers!…

'There was one consolation, to be sure. A famous organist, who had been invited to test the new instrument in the church, was not due to arrive until the day after the concert; I must confess that I had used a little cunning to arrange matters that way.

'Feeling rather more uneasy than usual, I entered our concert hall the next evening. It was so packed that even a few unaccompanied ladies could not find a seat. The songs with which we opened the concert went splendidly well, in their own modest way. Although our tenor was not on top form, we still had strengths that could have been the envy of many a larger singing club. The nightwatchman and our portly headmaster were a good pair of supporting basses; they amply filled in the gaps left by the thinner voices. The applause was enthusiastic. Singers and listeners of the little town were on the best of terms.

'And so the programme proceeded gradually towards the *Fantasy-Sonata*. As the applause for an attractive little song by Ludwig Berger – "*Als der Sandwirt von Passeier*"[9] – was dying down, I sat down at the piano, and an expectant silence came over the hall. I took a few deep breaths and opened the score. Then I cast a final fleeting glance out into the audience. The numerous staring faces out there kindled in me a kind of terror. Luckily I detected little Anna's brown eyes, which looked over at me, big and happy, and at that moment the many-headed monster was transformed into a sweetly benevolent being. I boldly struck a few chord progressions to herald the start of my performance. Then a thought rushed through my mind: "Sacred Master, grant that I may lay your golden notes in their hearts. May all of them, yes every one, be blessed by you!" And with that I began my Mozart, first the adagio. I truly believe I played well, for my mind was filled with the beauty of the work alone, and by an inspired impulse to communicate to others the joy of my own understanding. I believe to this day that my old teacher would have praised me; but she never attended live performances.

'I had already reached the last section of the andantino, when from here and there in the hall I sensed whispering between the notes. I was stunned; they weren't listening! It must be my fault, it could not be Mozart's. I started the allegro with a sense of foreboding, the more so because there was a passage in the second section which I had had to practise with particular care. But I recovered my calm: there were people out there to whom only trumpet music had any meaning. What were these people to me? One thing alone disturbed me; the fat headmaster had drawn closer and closer to me as I played. He might have any number of evil designs – perhaps he was going to trim the candles, and in the process drop the great brass trimmer on the keys, or maybe even turn the pages for me – something I could never tolerate anyone else doing. I played hurriedly to the end of the right-hand page, just to avoid having his fat hand get hold of the score too soon. That helped; he remained where he was, as if spellbound. Soon I had turned the page myself, and was playing confidently on, towards the troublesome passage. At this moment I heard the creak of a door below me in the hall, and could not help seeing all heads turn. More whispering, this time louder than before. I could not tell the reason, but I stopped breathing. And then I quite clearly heard a voice somewhere close to me saying, "But I thought he wasn't coming till tomorrow! What a pleasure for us all that he has come today!" So he had come after all! It was a stunning blow. What did I have to offer this man – this great artist – with my playing? Where could he be standing or sitting out there? From somewhere amidst all these hundreds of faces his eyes were watching me. And now – I actually felt it – he was inclining his head to take in every single one of my notes. A whole host of anxious thoughts raced through my head. My fingers felt paralysed all of a sudden, but attempted to play a few more bars. Then a helpless sense of indifference overwhelmed me and I was at that moment transported to another time and place far in the past. All at once I felt that the piano stood in its old place in my parents' living-room, and that beside me stood my father. Instead of the keys, I was reaching for his ghostly hand.

'I can scarcely say what happened next. When I came to my senses again I was sitting on a chair in a room behind the platform of the hall; it was where we used to take off our coats. I had felt unwell – at least that was what I believed I had said in the hall.

'A lamp with a long wick burned on the table. The dimly lit walls of the room, the assortment of dark clothes which lay everywhere – it was a desolate scene indeed. I had once sat like this as a child, though not so utterly crushed as now. And I felt that my eyes were dry, and there was no knock at the door – no one to send me to my father. I was a man now. "My poor, dear boy!" How long he had been dead, the man who had once spoken these words!

'I became aware of a confused clamour of voices over in the hall. I cannot say whether I had simply not heard it until now, or whether it was only at this moment that it broke out; but it struck me with sudden terror and chased me from the room and out of the building. Bare-headed and without my coat, I rushed out into the street and away, without looking back; out I went through the gateway and into the open. First came the old streets lined with lime trees, then the broad, deserted main road. I wandered further and further, without aim, without thought – except for a fear of the world and of people, raging in my head.

'Far beyond the town, the road passed over a hill which plunged precipitously down on one side. At the bottom flowed a rapid stream – I could hear the constant rush of water close by me. I can see it to this day: to the east was the thin crescent moon, casting no light but sharply incised in the gloomy night sky. On earth, darkness had fallen all around. Reaching the highest point, I noticed a large rock standing out over the water, under a tree. Without knowing why, I sat down on the stone. It was still early March; the branches above me were still bare, and struck against each other in the night breezes. Now and again droplets of water fell on my head and trickled coldly over my face. Behind me was the endless, monotonous rushing of the water below, enticing me to sleep like a lullaby.

'I leant my head against the damp trunk of the tree and listened to the seductive melody of the stream. "Yes!" I thought, "sleep, if one might but sleep!" And a voice seemed to arise and call up to me: "*Ach, unten, da unten die kühle Ruh.*"[10] The words and the sweet, melancholy music of Schubert penetrated my heart deeper and deeper. At this moment I heard footsteps from far off, and suddenly I leapt to my feet, as if awakened from sleep. Now I was no longer the poetical miller of the Schubert song, I was the son of a worthy, practical man. Once again, this was no time for silly notions!

'The steps approached me, nearer and nearer from the direction of the road, and with them I also heard other pattering feet like those of a small dog. There could no longer be any doubt: it was her, and with her was her little spaniel. So even now there was a human soul that had not forgotten me! My heart was in my mouth. Was it with joy or with fear that I could now deceive myself? But here, like a ray of light from out of the darkness, came her lovely young voice: "Herr Valentin! Is that you, Herr Valentin?"

'And I answered, ashamed: "Yes, Anna, of course it is. How do you come to be here?"

'Now she stood before me, and laid her hand on my arm. "I… asked in the town, and they said they'd seen you leaving through the gate."

'"But this is no place for you, all alone on a deserted road!"

'"I was so afraid. You were ill. Why on earth didn't you go home?"

'"No, Anna," I said, "I wasn't ill. That was just one of those lies that need or shame forces from our lips. It's just that I had taken on something which God has denied me the ability to do."

'Two little arms fell about my neck, and Anna's innocent little head lay sobbing on my breast. "Just look at you!" she whispered. "No hat on your head, no coat!"

'"Yes, Anna, I suppose I forgot them when I rushed out."

'Her little hands clasped me more tightly. It was so still out there in the dark expanse of the fields. The little dog lay down at our feet. It might have seemed to any eye watching us there together that we were sealing a lifelong bond between us. And yet, it was a parting.'

As he uttered these words, the old man stared subdued into the glass which he had just picked up, as if the dreams of his youth might now rise from its depths. One side of the window casement stood open, and through it the call of a bird flying overhead sounded from the sky.

He looked up. 'Did you hear that?' he said. 'That night too, it was just such a call from the birds of passage that drove us home. We walked all the way, still hand in hand.

'The next morning old Signora Caterina came down to me from her attic eyrie. She was quite beside herself: "And in front of all those provincials!" she cried. "It's just that you haven't learnt how to come on stage, Monsieur Valentin. Look, this is how *I* entered the spotlight in my day!" And she stood, wrapped in her shawl, and struck a heroic pose in front of me. "I would just like to see the person who could have silenced *me* when I sang! Even before the great master himself I only trembled a little bit!"

'But what help was this to me? What was more, that day I learnt that my old fellow-pupil was also to establish himself in the town as a music teacher. Perhaps his virtuosity had waned after all, but he still had what I lacked, and I knew for sure that it was time for me to go.

'Only a few days later little Anna helped me pack my trunks, and her compassionate eyes wept many a tear over my old books; in the end it was I who had to comfort her!

'I had little doubt where I should direct my steps. Here in the town of my birth it is true I had no house or home, but just outside the gates was my parents' grave. When I arrived here and unpacked my things once more from the trunks, I found hidden among my music scores the familiar little crystal box, filled to the brim with peppermint pastilles. The good Signora Caterina – she, if no one else, had wished to award me the prize of honour!

'But it is late,' he said, suddenly standing up and taking from his pocket a large gold watch. 'Long past decent citizens' bedtime! What will my old bleacher and his folk think?'

'And little Anna?' I asked. 'What became of her?'

He was at this moment busy replacing the long pipe on the hook from which I had taken it down for him. He turned towards me, and on his face was that gentle, childlike smile that gave him such grace.

'What became of little Anna?' he repeated. 'She became just what a spirited young girl always should become – a serious wife and mother! Having made our signora's painful final withdrawal from this world's stage a little more comfortable – by truly caring for her, I have no doubt – she did not find her prince, to be sure, but she did fulfil one of her humbler promises to her old friend; she married a worthy schoolmaster. They have lived here in the town for years. When we met earlier, I had just come from their house.'

'So little Anna is the mother of your favourite pupil!'

He nodded. 'Life has dealt with me tolerably well, hasn't it? But for now, I wish you goodnight. Don't forget the Bürger!' And he took his grey hat and left.

I went to the open window and called after him 'Goodnight!' as he stepped out through the door below. My eyes followed him as he hurried down the street between the dim lamps and finally disappeared in the darkness.

The stillness of night had now descended all around. Between the shadows of the earth and the dark depths of the sky, human life lay slumbering, with all its unsolved puzzles.

Around a week later I found myself on my way to the little house of the bleacher. I had not yet reached the place when I heard coming from the house the sound of piano-playing. 'Ah,' I thought, 'now you'll find him completely engrossed in his Mozart!' But when I came through the open front door and went and stood outside my friend's room, what I heard being played inside was one of Schubert's *Moments Musicaux* – and it was not a man's hands that were playing.

'Portamento, not staccato!' said my friend's voice.

Another, younger voice with a particularly pure ring to it, answered: 'I know, Uncle, but doesn't the staccato sound much much nicer here?'

'Oh, you little dreamer!' I heard. 'First, *you* write something like that; then you can play it however you like!'

There was a little pause; then followed a portamento, and I could see clearly in my mind how those young fingers carried the melody from one key to the next.

'Now do it again, just to make sure it's really secure.'

And I heard it again, and it was perfectly secure.

On the door in front of me was a little notice, apparently new:

And she was well! How could I not praise God?
The earth is now so fair,
But glorious too, as is his heaven above,
And fine to wander there!

The verse was from the *Wandsbecker Bote*[11]; I knew it well, but this time my friend Valentin had taken the liberty of making a slight change, for it was only of his own return to health that old Asmus had spoken in the original poem.

Reflecting on the verses, I opened the door and saw a young girl, still a child, sitting next to Valentin at the piano and looking up at him with large, attentive eyes.

With his charming, and now mildly self-conscious smile, he stood up.

'Did you find our recent little session together agreeable?' I asked, holding out my hand.

'Did I?' he replied. 'Oh, yes, it was excellent. And you? I probably spoke a great deal – you know how it is when two people share a good glass together!' He said this almost in a whisper, and rather as if he felt he must excuse himself; his pale blue eyes were directed towards me, and in them was an indescribable expression of tenderness.

'On the contrary,' I said. 'I am still not satisfied! You will have to tell me much more. But,' I added in a lower voice, 'first you must finish your lesson with your favourite pupil – that's her for certain! Meanwhile I'll look for the Bürger on your book shelf.'

He nodded eagerly, 'We'll be finished very shortly!' and returned to his pupil.

I searched among his little treasures, and soon came upon the two Chodowiecki Bürgers, one of which I took at random off the shelf for myself. While I was contemplating the title page, on which the great ballad-writer appears in a full wig playing a harp, and at the same time the *Moments Musicaux* were sounding in my ears, a maidservant entered the room with coffee and a plate of cakes.

She spread out a pure white cloth on the side-table and put the coffee-service down. Two blue and white cups stood alongside the Bunzlau coffee-pot, but after a discreet sign from Valentin a third cup appeared. I had seen this, but my attention was then suddenly seized by a poem I found written on the white flyleaf of my little book. The lines were youthful and innocent, and yet they seemed to blow gently upon me like the breath of spring:

O thou divine and lovely world,
Thou hast my heart with radiance fill'd!
All was before so strange and stark:
Thy sunlight now dispels the dark.
The grass breathes fragrance everywhere,

A bird with singing fills the air:
Let him whose heart is pure and strong
With joyful spirit join my song!'
And I did then my song impart,
Knowing that strength within my heart!

I read the lines again and again; so this was the poem he had written among the violets; Valentin, the whole person, was there – that was exactly how I knew him, and that was how the young man must once have been.

And there he stood before me in person holding the hand of the slim, pale young girl with the gleaming brown hair. 'Yes,' he said. 'This is my Marie; today we are enjoying our Sunday afternoon once more. And, truly, it gives me such great pleasure that you too have come to join us.' Then he saw the book with the inscribed page in my hand, and suddenly blushed like a young girl. 'Take the other copy for yourself,' he said, 'the print is much clearer.'

But I tried to hang on to my possession. 'May I not keep this one? Or will you not be parted from it? I see you had it when you were a boy.'

He looked at me with an expression almost of gratitude. 'Do you really mean it?' he said. 'In that case it's in good hands – in the best possible hands!'

We sat, the three of us, around our Sunday coffee-table; the little lady played hostess with grace, but otherwise listened in silence to our conversation.

'Well, Valentin my friend,' I said, 'there is something else you must tell me; for this dark brew can also open men's lips. What became of your field of violets? Does the spring sun still look down on it, or has it gone the way of so much else that is beautiful – and been turned into a potato patch?'

Over Valentin's face crept a cheerful, even slightly crafty smile. 'You obviously don't yet realise,' he said, 'that I am a secret spendthrift!'

'Oh ho, my friend!'

'Yes, it's true! The place belonged to an eccentric old fellow. I became his heir; that is, from his estate I purchased this useless piece of land for some bright silver coins. But, Marie,' and here he nodded to his little favourite, 'we both know its true worth, don't we? – and we also know whose birthday we must pick those violets for!'

The slim girl laid her head on his shoulder and threw her arms round his neck. 'For Mother's birthday,' she said, softly. 'But Uncle, that's still a long way off.'

'Well, well, spring will come again!'

'God willing, Herr Valentin,' I said. 'Might I go with you, and help make the garland?'

Two hands stretched out towards me; one was slim and beautiful and young, the other – this one, I know, was a true and faithful one.

I did not go with them. Even before the end of that winter, my life took me far away from the town. Only once did I receive a message of greeting from Valentin, through a common acquaintance. Once or twice more, when spring came, I thought of his garden of violets, and then no more. Other shapes thronged into my mind, and behind them the form of the quiet musician gradually disappeared completely.

Some ten years later I was making a long journey, and I passed through one of the larger central German towns, one whose orchestral society enjoyed a well-earned reputation even in wider circles. This was due not only to its own very competent performances; the directors also managed, even with the limited resources they had, to attract for almost every concert some distinguished artist from outside.

It was a day in late autumn, and already evening, when I arrived. A music-loving friend who lived there had waited for me at the station. He informed me that there was an orchestral concert that evening; I should go with him immediately, as there was no time to spare. I knew from previous experience that there was no contradicting this enthusiast, and so I handed over my luggage ticket, along with some surplus travelling effects, to a servant of one of the hotels. Straight away, we got into a carriage that took us, on payment of double fares, at rapid speed to the 'Museum', which was already known to me. On the way, I learnt that for this concert a young lady singer had been engaged – a unique talent in classical music who had an eccentric way of always presenting herself as the pupil of a wholly unknown master.

The concert had already started when we arrived, and we had to wait behind the closed door of the hall until the final bars of the *Hebrides Overture*[12] had died away. When the doors were opened again, my friend stuffed a programme he had procured in the meantime into the breast pocket of my coat, then led me by the arm into the packed hall. It was not long before he had somehow managed to make two seats free for us. Next to me sat an old white-haired gentleman with two dark eyes set amid the fine contours of his face. 'So, now to Mozart!' he said under his breath, and folded his hands on a yellow silk handkerchief which he had spread over his knees.

Soon after, while under the bright light of the gas lamps I was contemplating the walls of the concert hall, which were decorated simply but with an unusual sense of colour, the singer appeared over on the platform – a young girl with a pale complexion and dark ringlets around her temples. The orchestra played the opening bars of Elvira's aria from the second act of 'Don Giovanni', and the singer raised the score in her hands: '*In quali eccessi, o numi!*'[13]

I felt I had never before heard a singer so unpretentious and yet so stirring. The old gentleman at my side nodded his head more and more approvingly; this was art which transmuted all the suffering of the world into melody! But then, as is always the way with beauty, it was over in a moment, just as the ear was most intoxicated by the sound.

A few piercing cheers of 'Bravo' flew through the hall together with some isolated clapping. The applause was by no means universal. A young man sitting in front of us turned his stylishly coifed head back towards the old man. 'What do you think, Uncle? Nice voice, but just a little strange? Self-taught!'

The old man looked at him discerningly. 'I see, dear nephew,' he said. 'So you could detect that, could you?' And turning to me with a courteous gesture he added, with a certain solemnity, 'That was Mozart as I used to hear him sung in my youth!'

The concert continued. 'Now we'll hear some of the society's own artistic endeavours,' the friend on my other side whispered in my ear.

And that was indeed the case. A string quartet by a living composer was played. None of the musicians' scrupulous care and accuracy was able to inspire the hearts of these connoisseurs; throughout the hall they could be seen looking around wearily, aimlessly. More than once the old Mozartian beside me had to suppress a fit of yawning behind his yellow silk handkerchief. At last the third and final movement had skipped along past us in its five-eight rhythm.

The players left the platform, and the music stands were cleared away. It was apparent from the largely vacant expressions in the auditorium that the audience had no idea what to make of this music. At this point the young singer returned to the platform with a score in her hand. Her face bore a mischievous, almost triumphant expression. I suspected for a moment that she was going to follow the modern antics of the strings with an even bolder display of the *vox humana*.

Fortunately I was proved wrong. This time there was not even an orchestral accompaniment; the conductor sat at the piano, which in the meantime had been brought to the front of the stage. He prefaced the performance with a few chords, and then began a prelude, as simple as it was sweetly melodic. A sudden sense of joyous revelation swept through the entire hall, and with the calm authority of the human voice the words came forth:

> '*O thou divine and lovely world,*
> *That hast my heart with radiance fill'd!*'

What was this? I knew these words; they were written on the blank paper at the front of my Bürger. These were the words of my old music master, Christian Valentin. Dear God, how long since I had thought of him!

The room was filled with the pure, youthful sounds, and I was overcome by indescribable emotion. Had he himself also written the melody for his poem? There stood the young singer, the score hanging in her hand; her young face spoke of rapture, of dedication and love. The last words of the song rang out with unutterable beauty:

> '*And I did then my song impart,*
> *Knowing that strength within my heart!*'

Deep silence reigned in the hall when she had finished singing. Then came tumultuous applause, which seemed as if it would never end. The old gentleman beside me had grasped my hand without my noticing, and now he pressed it tenderly. 'That is what we call soul – yes, soul!' he said, and shook his grey head. I hastily snatched the programme from my pocket. Sure enough, here was the name of my friend. It appeared twice, first alongside that of the young singer, who named him as her teacher, and then again as the composer of the song that had so overwhelmed and inspired the audience.

I stood up and looked around, as if somewhere among the audience I would discover him in person, his beloved old face and that charming, youthful smile still playing upon it. It was an illusion; my old friend had not been there to listen to the sweet song of his boyhood, though its joy and calm could still be seen in the faces of those who had heard it. For me it was as if I had, after all, been with my quiet master where his violets grew.

I was hardly aware of the rest of the concert, but later, as I lay like a tortured man on the hateful incline of my hotel bed, I was consoled by the lovely lingering tones of the song, until at last I fell asleep; those sweet sounds rang again and again in my ear, like the voice of children through the October storm that raged outside the windows. And at the same time the young singer's pale face floated before my closed eyes.

So something had come of my friend's music after all. All the old Signora Caterina's art rang from this young creature with bell-like clarity. For there was not a single doubt in my mind who it was I had heard singing, though I no longer remembered this doubly beloved child at all clearly, nor had I ever come to know her surname. Nor shall I record it here. It is true that at that time she had made something of a name for herself; indeed, for a short time she even caused some controversy, setting the old and the new musical worlds at odds with each other. Soon, however, she sank from notice and became once more one of the great majority whose joys and sufferings are lived out in smaller circles without exciting attention.

My first thought the following morning was of course to seek her out and obtain some word of my almost forgotten friend; but I was prevented from doing so by some unforeseen business. The friend who had dragged me to the concert with such determination, and after it had somewhat ungraciously abandoned me, now came to my help. My meeting with the singer took place in his house that evening.

Many guests were gathered there. I soon noticed that they were without exception music-lovers of the truest kind. The old Mozartian was among them, and I was privileged to shake hands with him most warmly.

And there she stood in person, chatting amiably with the pretty young daughter of the household, to whom she was apparently an object of great admiration. After I had greeted the lady of the house, my friend introduced me to her; as he did so, she put her arm round the child and drew her gently to her side. For a moment she looked searchingly into my face, and then held out her hand.

'It is true, isn't it?' I said. 'It really is you? Did we not once spend a Sunday afternoon together?'

She smiled and nodded. 'I have not forgotten. My old friend and teacher often spoke of you, especially when the spring came. You wanted to come with us to see his violets.'

'I feel,' I replied softly, 'that you and I, at least, visited that place together last night.'

With an affectionate look she replied, 'So you were at the concert? Oh, I am so happy to know that!' We fell silent for a moment while she leant down to the child who was still clinging to her.

'You stated in the programme that you were his pupil. It is not normally the custom for artists to share their fame like this with an old teacher.'

She blushed deeply. 'Oh, no,' she cried, 'that was very far from my thoughts! I don't know why I did it. It just seemed obvious – I feel even now that he holds my hand. I have so much to thank him for!'

'But he,' I answered, 'our Master Valentin, what did *he* think?'

She looked at me with her calm eyes. 'That is what I meant,' she said, 'he is no longer with us; he passed away long ago.'

And neither did I see the young singer again. I like to think she found happiness years ago as a mother. In the evening hours, when work has ended and the calm of night is beginning to descend, perhaps she opens the piano and sings to her children that sweet lark's song of her friend who died long ago.

And that too is a cherished memory.

NOTES

THE LAKE OF THE BEES

1. The Lake of the Bees.

A QUIET MUSICIAN

1. Wilhelm Hauff (1802–27) was a German poet, novelist and writer of fairy tales. His greatest work *Lichtenstein* (1826) is widely regarded as the first German historical novel.
2. Ludwig Uhland (1787–1862) was an important Romantic poet and playwright and one of the founders of German literary scholarship and philology; Ludwig Hölty (1748–76) was a poet of the Göttingen circle, whose work was inspired by the German folk-song tradition and focused largely on the subject of nature.
3. The landscape painter Carl Friedrich Lessing (1808–80) was the grand-nephew of the great poet and critic Gotthold Ephraim Lessing (1729–81).
4. Daniel Chodowiecki (1726–1801) was a highly popular Prussian painter and engraver.
5. Gottfried August Bürger (1747–94) was a German poet noted for the folkish style of his work; his best-known work is the Gothic *Lenore* (1773).
6. Singing societies; male-voice choirs.
7. Dear friend (Italian).
8. From the beginning (musical direction; Italian).
9. Ludwig Berger (1777–1838) was a Prussian-born composer of songs, cantatas, unfinished operas and piano music; he is principally remembered as the teacher of Mendelssohn. The song '*Als der Sandwirt von Passeier*' ('As the innkeeper from Passeier…') concerns the Tyrolean patriot Andreas Hofer (1767–1810), who, from humble beginnings as the landlord of the Sandhof inn, rose to lead the Tyroleans in 1809 against the Bavarian rule and the French occupation of the same year.
10. 'Ah, beneath, there beneath, there is cool and calm'; the words are from the poem '*Der Müller und der Bach*' ('The Miller and the Brook') by Wilhelm Müller (1794–1827), which was set to music by Schubert in 1823.
11. *Wandsbecker Bote* ('Wandsbeck Messenger') was a series of poems originally published in the Hamburg newspaper of the same name. The poems were written by Matthias Claudius (1740–1815), who edited and republished them in book form between 1774 and 1812.
12. The *Hebrides Overture* (1832), by Mendelssohn (1809–47), was composed after a visit to Fingal's Cave in Scotland.
13. 'In what excesses, oh gods!…'; the aria is from *Don Giovanni*, Act II, Scene 14.

BIOGRAPHICAL NOTE

Theodor Storm was born in 1817 in Husum, in the duchy of Schleswig. His father was a lawyer, and came from a family of prominent public officials. Storm was educated in Husum and Lübeck where he studied the German classics and was particularly influenced by the poetry of Heinrich Heine. In 1836, while still at school, Storm met and became attached to ten-year-old Bertha von Buchan, for whom he wrote poetry and stories; a relationship that prefigured that of Reinhard and Elisabeth in *The Lake of the Bees*.

In 1837 Storm entered the University of Kiel to study jurisprudence. He continued his writing, however, and formed several lasting literary friendships. Storm returned to Husum after university, where he established his own solicitor's practice in 1843. Marriage to his cousin, Constanze Esmarch, followed in 1846 – his relationship with Bertha von Buchan having broken down four years earlier. Storm's home life was at times turbulent; he was a notably strict father to his eight children, and his troubled relationship with his eldest son Hans – whilst inspiring Storm's 1878 story *Carsten Curator* – contributed to the latter's early death from alcoholism.

During the late 1840s Storm became involved with the Schleswig-Holstein Freedom Movement. He also began to write patriotic poetry and was signatory to a number of petitions and letters of protest, and his prominence in the anti-Danish movement led to the withdrawal in 1852 of his right to practise law in Schleswig. Storm was forced to move to Prussia, where he continued to work in low-paid positions, but also began to form important friendships with other writers, in particular with Paul Heyse and Theodor Fontane. Storm's sense of home and belonging – a theme that recurs in his literature – was strong, however, and he was quick to return to Husum in 1864 after the liberation of the duchies by Austro-Prussian forces. The inhabitants welcomed him back and he was made a district magistrate. He remained in Schleswig-Holstein through the Prussian annexation of 1866 and continued in public service for another fourteen years. Storm died from cancer in 1888.

Jonathan Katz is a musician, musicologist and linguist. He is Head of the Classics department at Westminster School, London, where for many years he was Master of the Queen's Scholars. Formerly he was a Research Fellow of Wolfson College, Oxford.

HESPERUS PRESS – 100 PAGES

Hesperus Press, as suggested by the Latin motto, is committed to bringing near what is far – far both in space and time. Works written by the greatest authors, and unjustly neglected or simply little known in the English-speaking world, are made accessible through new translations and a completely fresh editorial approach. Through these short classic works, each around 100 pages in length, the reader will be introduced to the greatest writers from all times and all cultures.

For more information on Hesperus Press, please visit our website: **www.hesperuspress.com**

ET REMOTISSIMA PROPE

SELECTED TITLES FROM HESPERUS PRESS

Gustave Flaubert *Memoirs of a Madman*
Alexander Pope *Scriblerus*
Ugo Foscolo *Last Letters of Jacopo Ortis*
Anton Chekhov *The Story of a Nobody*
Joseph von Eichendorff *Life of a Good-for-nothing*
Mark Twain *The Diary of Adam and Eve*
Giovanni Boccaccio *Life of Dante*
Victor Hugo *The Last Day of a Condemned Man*
Joseph Conrad *Heart of Darkness*
Edgar Allan Poe *Eureka*
Emile Zola *For a Night of Love*
Daniel Defoe *The King of Pirates*
Giacomo Leopardi *Thoughts*
Nikolai Gogol *The Squabble*
Franz Kafka *Metamorphosis*
Herman Melville *The Enchanted Isles*
Leonardo da Vinci *Prophecies*
Charles Baudelaire *On Wine and Hashish*
William Makepeace Thackeray *Rebecca and Rowena*
Wilkie Collins *Who Killed Zebedee?*
Théophile Gautier *The Jinx*
Charles Dickens *The Haunted House*
Luigi Pirandello *Loveless Love*
Fyodor Dostoevsky *Poor People*
E.T.A. Hoffmann *Mademoiselle de Scudéri*
Henry James *In the Cage*
Francis Petrarch *My Secret Book*
André Gide *Theseus*
D.H. Lawrence *The Fox*
Percy Bysshe Shelley *Zastrozzi*

Marquis de Sade *Incest*
Oscar Wilde *The Portrait of Mr W.H.*
Giacomo Casanova *The Duel*
Leo Tolstoy *Hadji Murat*
Friedrich von Schiller *The Ghost-seer*
Nathaniel Hawthorne *Rappaccini's Daughter*
Pietro Aretino *The School of Whoredom*
Honoré de Balzac *Colonel Chabert*
Thomas Hardy *Fellow-Townsmen*
Arthur Conan Doyle *The Tragedy of the Korosko*
Katherine Mansfield *In a German Pension*
Stendhal *Memoirs of an Egotist*
Giovanni Verga *Life in the Country*
Ivan Turgenev *Faust*
F. Scott Fitzgerald *The Rich Boy*
Dante Alighieri *New Life*
Guy de Maupassant *Butterball*
Charlotte Brontë *The Green Dwarf*
Elizabeth Gaskell *Lois the Witch*
Joris-Karl Huysmans *With the Flow*
George Eliot *Amos Barton*
Gabriele D'Annunzio *The Book of the Virgins*
Heinrich von Kleist *The Marquise of O–*
Alexander Pushkin *Dubrovsky*